The Leaders of the Old Bar in Philadelphia

Horace Binney

The Leaders of the Old Bar in Philadelphia

Reprint of the original, first published in 1859.

1st Edition 2023 | ISBN: 978-3-37514-018-2

Verlag (Publisher): Salzwasser Verlag GmbH, Zeilweg 44, 60439 Frankfurt, Deutschland
Vertretungsberechtigt (Authorized to represent): E. Roepke, Zeilweg 44, 60439 Frankfurt, Deutschland
Druck (Print): Books on Demand GmbH, In de Tarpen 42, 22848 Norderstedt, Deutschland

THE LEADERS

OF THE

OLD BAR OF PHILADELPHIA.

"One touch of Nature makes the whole world kin,—
That all, with one consent, praise new-born gauds,
Though they are made and moulded of things past,
And give to dust that is a little gilt
More laud than gilt o'erdusted."

PHILADELPHIA:
PRINTED BY C. SHERMAN & SON.
1859.

PREFACE.

In the title of these sketches, the "Old Bar of Philadelphia," refers to the first Bar after the Declaration of Independence.

Of the primitive Bar of the Province, we know nothing; and next to nothing of the men who appeared at it from time to time, up to the termination of the Colonial government. The statement of Chief Justice Tilghman, in the Bush Hill case,* reveals to us all we know, and all that probably we can ever know, in regard to this subject; for, as the grandson of Tench Francis, who was Attorney-General in 1745, and connected by marriage and association with the most eminent families of the Bar, he knew as much of the former Bar as any of his cotemporaries, and they have all long since departed without adding anything to what he left. "From what I have been able to learn," said the Chief Justice, "of the early history of Pennsylvania, it was a long time before she possessed any lawyers of eminence. There were never wanting men of strong minds, very well able to conduct the business of the Courts, without much regard to form. Such, in particular, was Andrew Hamilton, the immediate predecessor of Mr. Francis, and the father of the testator; but Mr. Francis appears to have been the first of our lawyers who mastered the technical difficulties of the profession. His precedents of pleadings have been handed down to the present day; and his commonplace book, which is in my possession, is an evidence

---

* Lyle v. Richards, 9 Serg. & Rawle.

of his great industry and accuracy." "Mr. Francis succeeded Mr. Hamilton, and Mr. Chew succeeded to Mr. Francis, in the office of Attorney-General, and in professional eminence."

Mr. Chew remained at the Bar until 1774, and was Chief Justice of the Supreme Court from that time until the former order of things passed away; and although there are a few other names, at the same epoch, to be added to these three, yet the narrowness of the tradition, taken altogether, the constitution of the Provincial Supreme Court, in which the Chief Justice was commonly the only lawyer, the total absence of every note of judicial decision until 1754, and the all but total until after 1776, had caused that Bar to disappear from nearly all memories at the beginning of the present century; and therefore, in the middle of the fourth generation since the Revolution, I have taken the liberty of referring to the earliest Bar under the new order of things, as being the Old Bar of Philadelphia. From that time to the present, the Bar of this City has been an identity, superintended by competent and frequently very able judges, whose proceedings have been vouched by authoritative reports, and having, at all times, among its leaders, men of legal erudition and ability. It is not, however, to ignore the primitive Bar, so much as to give its due precedence to the first Bar of the Commonwealth as a scientific Bar, and as the true ancestry of the present Bar, that I have used the language in the title-page.

The description of the subjects of sketch, as *the* leaders of the Bar, may appear to be too definite; but although definite, it is not meant to be exclusive. It must not imply that there were no others who held the position of leaders. The three in particular were the seniors, by a few years, of all the Bar, and were generally the most prominent in the professional as well as in the public eye. My own freer association with them has induced me to select them from the body, and to pay to them a debt which, though it may have too little dignity to be called a debt to the law, is a debt or duty to their learning and ability in the law. In the new order of things introduced by the American Revolution, these gentlemen largely contributed to establish the reputation of the Bar of this City. Their professional example and learning were of great and extensive use in their day, and ought to be handed down by something better than such fugitive pages as these.

A lawyer who has passed his youth and early manhood in the society of such men, is the happier for it through life, and especially in old age. On all occasions of vexation or weariness with things near at hand, he can escape at pleasure into the past of these men, which was full of their influence, full also of judicial independence and dignity, and full of professional honor, with unlimited public respect; from which scene, the few clouds that are to be found in the clearest skies have been absorbed or dispelled by time, and to which the clouds of his own day, if there are any, cannot follow him.

H. B.

PHILADELPHIA, March, 1859.

WILLIAM LEWIS.

WILLIAM LEWIS.

It may be thought that I select a very narrow and local theme, when I attempt to sketch some of the personal and professional characteristics of a lawyer of the Philadelphia Bar, who was little more than a lawyer, though he was a great lawyer, and who culminated in his profession more than sixty years since. But I adopt the theme, in some degree, because it is narrow and local, and is therefore more within my compass; and because it is beyond the memory of most of the living, and therefore, in the advantages of personal recollection, is pretty much an octogenarian perquisite of my own. What I write upon the subject, cannot be of any general interest. It is too remote, and too limited. It wants the essential, and, at this day, all-engrossing attractions of the new and the various or diversified; and it will want, what alone can supply the place of these attractions, a treatment that is a substitute for the subject. But it is a debt that I would pay; the joint debt, perhaps, of several, which has fallen, according to law, upon the longest liver; and I would pay it for them and for myself. A general interest in the transaction is therefore comparatively indifferent to me. I expect, consequently, that no one out of the Pennsylvania Bar, and very few who are not of the Philadelphia Bar, will look at it; and, except to this Bar, I offer neither invitation nor inducement to put aside for it, even for an hour, the more stimulant interests of the day.

Has not the modern race of lawyers everywhere undergone some change from the old times, by rising or falling into the Athenian category,—the very large class of those who spend their time in telling or hearing some new thing? There are, at least, professional tendencies that way, which make them less and less curious of anything that savors of a former age. Most of the old limitations have been abridged, and the exceptions to them cut away, to save the labor of looking back. Old authorities no longer divide with old wine, the reverence of either seniors or juniors. Most of the old law books, that used to be thought almost as good a foundation for their part of the truth, as the prophets and apostles are for the whole truth, are taken away, I rather think, from the bottom of the building, and thrown into the garret. That Littleton *upon* whom Coke sits, or seems to sit to the end of things, as Carlisle says, has fewer than of old, I suspect, to sit with him for long hours to alleviate the incumbrance. For the most part, as I am told, the incumbent and the succumbent lie together in the dust, which uppermost not many care to know. All the *Entries*, Brooke, and Coke, and Levinz, and Rastall, and the others, have made their *exits* some time ago, and will not appear again before the epilogue. Almost any law book that is more than twenty-one years of age, like a single lady who has attained that climacter, is said to be too old for much devotion. Indexes, Digests, and Treatises, which supply thoughts without cultivating the power of thinking, and are renewed with notes and commentaries *de die in diem*, to spare the fatigue of research, are supposed to be the best current society for student as well as for practitioner. Such are the rumors which float upon the air. "Old things are passed away, all things are new,"—a great truth in its own sense when it was first spoken, and always—is now thought to be true in all senses, and renewable from year to year, forever; and lawyers give as ready a welcome to new things, and turn as cold a shoulder to the old, as the rest of the world. Such is the apprehension.

I ought therefore to be, and am, very shy about writing anything upon an antiquated subject, with even an apparent direction to this body of men generally; and therefore I repeat that I do not expect the perusal of what I write, either in regard to the very strong and accomplished lawyer whose name is at the head of my page, or of the two whose names are to follow, by any but a few of the lawyers of the Philadelphia Bar, either themselves senescent, and in the practice of turning their eyes occasionally backwards as well as forwards, or some young lawyer, who bears in his veins some of the blood of the old Bar; and if the latter description shall do me that honor, I may give him a useful reminder of the oblivion that has fallen upon some of the ablest of the profession, and which will come upon him some day, though he shall live to be among the most able. He may be led, perhaps, to seek an antidote for the apprehension; and I can assure him that he will have no difficulty in finding it, if he "seek diligently."

At the age of the American world in which Mr. Lewis lived, or rather in which he came to adult age and character in his profession, there was no crowd of cities in our country to prevent a marked local reputation at the Bar of a particular city, from passing freely through the length and breadth of the inhabited land; or from being enlarged by the mist of distance, as is universally the case in such a condition of society. It happened in that day, and probably from this circumstance, that from Maryland to Massachusetts, there was, in several of the States, some one name at the Bar which, in the view of persons removed a few hundred miles, loomed very large, and overshadowed all other lawyers in the same State. Theophilus Parsons at Boston, Luther Martin at Baltimore, and William Lewis at Philadelphia, were respectively such overshadowing names. In one or two of the instances, the shadow disappeared altogether in coming up to the object; for, at that point, names of less general mark were found to be free from all eclipse. In all, perhaps, the shadow was, by the same approach, reduced to a penumbra. Mr. Parsons, of Boston, was regarded, in Philadelphia, as the first and comparatively the only great lawyer in Massachusetts. In Boston, Mr. Dexter, who was also a great lawyer, was considered his equal in intellectual powers, as indeed he was equal to any one; but in maturity and fulness of legal learning, Parsons was held to be the first. The same, perhaps, may be said in regard to Mr. Martin and one or more of his brethren at the Maryland Bar. Nearly the same of Mr. Lewis. But although Mr. Lewis was the senior of the Philadelphia Bar, and was in reality a very able as well as eminent lawyer, his reputation was, from accidental circumstances, more transcendent abroad than at home. It was very great at home; but there was at least one at his side who, in some respects, stood out in a clearer light before the members of his own Bar, and one or two others who were near to them, by what Iago calls " the old gradation, where each second stood heir to the first."

There was, at the same period, as great learning and eminence at the Bar of New York, as at any of the Bars of the country; but the greatest name at that Bar did not belong exclusively, nor even principally, to the Bar; and the fame which had followed the greater relations of his military and political life, drew distant attention away from the professional talents which at that time adorned the Bar of New York. Such a man as Richard Harrison would have been deemed a great lawyer anywhere. Mr. Vanvechten, of Albany, of the old Dutch stock, stood like a sea-wall of the old country, against the irruption of any bad law into the causes he sustained. But both these gentlemen were better known at home than abroad. For large and original speculation, Hamilton was a greater lawyer than either of them; but in legal erudition, perhaps, not the equal of either. Hamilton's considerable and very available learning in the law, was overshadowed by his learning in public or political law, by his versatile talents, by his marvellous powers of formation and order in war and government, and by the great relations, military and civil, in which he stood to the country. I am not aware, therefore, of anything, accidental or otherwise, which caused any one name at the Bar of New York, in the last century, to loom so large, in the distance, in its professional dimensions, as to prejudice the pretensions of other names at the same Bar.

This distant reputation was by no means a decisive test of superiority at the Bar. It proceeded as often from great public interest in the questions with which the advocate had grappled successfully, as it did from his own general ability and learning.

There is some proof of this in the reputation of Andrew Hamilton, of whom a word from Chief Justice Tilghman has been said in the Preface. He was not a scientific or thoroughly trained lawyer; but he gained almost unlimited fame by his defence of John Peter Zenger, in the Supreme Court of New York, upon an information of libel, in the year 1734. It was the spirit of Independence, even at that early day in the Colonies, that lifted him up to general admiration, and to professional distinction. And yet his argument, which we have, it is said, from his own pen, treats of no such topic. He merely claimed to liberate the jury from the authority of some disagreeable law, and of an obnoxious Court holding its appointment from the Crown. No lawyer can read that argument without perceiving, that, while it was a spirited and vigorous, though rather overbearing, harangue, which carried the jury away from the instruction of the Court, and from the established law of both the Colony and the Mother Country, he argued elaborately what was not law anywhere, with the same confidence as he did the better points of his case. It is, however, worth remembering, and to his honor, that he was half a century before Mr. Erskine, and the Declaratory Act of Mr. Fox, in asserting the right of the jury to give a general verdict in libel as much as in murder; and, in spite of the Court, the jury believed him, and acquitted his client.

I was familiar with the praise of Mr. Parsons, in Massachusetts, while I was receiving my education at Cambridge, and am still thankful for the opportunity I enjoyed of witnessing, in the Supreme Court of that State, in a session at Cambridge, for the County of Middlesex, in 1795 or 1796, an exhibition of intellectual gladiature of the brightest kind, between Parsons, as counsel for one Claflin, indicted of blasphemy under a statute of Massachusetts, and James Sullivan, the Attorney-General of the State. The wide reputation of Mr. Parsons was in no respect accidental.

The Court was held by Dana, Chief Justice, Paine, Sumner, and Dawes, Justices. The blasphemy I will not repeat, but it gave Mr. Parsons an occasion or opportunity of showing up some of the supposed phases of Calvinistic theology, or, more accurately, some of the opinions or statements of writers supposed to be of that school, which gave countenance, he thought, to what was charged against Claflin as blasphemy, and were, if anything, rather worse. I supposed, at the time, that there was no other help for Claflin; and I dare say that, bad as any blasphemy may be, there may be found in some extreme views of very different schools of theology, something quite as bad. But the marvel was, to see the promptness and acuteness with which Parsons repeated, explained, applied, and enforced his citations in the best form for his client. My imagination fired at the spectacle of this *omnis homo*, as well-furnished in theology as in law, and of as much repute for Greek as for English, Socratic in his subtlety, and not otherwise in his careless dress, his purple Bandana handkerchief curled loosely over his neckcloth, and his reddish-brown scratch, something awry,—he all the while pouring from under it the doctrines he had culled, and weaving them up with the subtlest ingenuity, to make a covering broad enough for Claflin. It was a glory of the Bar. But the stiff old Statute was too much for him. I think I recollect a part of Claflin's sentence, so strange to the ear of a Pennsylvania lawyer —that he should sit an hour *upon* the gallows, with the rope round his neck! Barring the rope, I should have been willing to sit there for two, not for blasphemy, nor alongside of Claflin, but to hear a repetition of Parsons. When I returned to Philadelphia, I was not surprised at the reputation which there surrounded the name of Theophilus Parsons.

WILLIAM LEWIS was a native of Chester County, in the State of Pennsylvania, where his birth took place about the year 1745. Both of these facts, however, rest upon early report, rather than upon authentic record. His condition in early life was that of the sons of country people generally, at that time. He used to say, as I have heard, that he had driven wagon in his early manhood; and I know that he was very proud of his skill in driving a pair of spirited horses to his phaeton at an advanced period of his life. His early education was no doubt imperfect; but by the force of strong native powers he acquired, pretty much by self-teaching, a good English education; and while he was studying law in the office of Nicholas Waln, an eminent Quaker and highly respectable lawyer, he mastered enough of Latin and French to read the old Entries and Reports, and he read them faithfully. His literary tincture was light. I rather suspect that it did not amount to what may be called the middle tincture, now pretty common among us; but all his life, after I knew him, he was something of a purist in language, and very exact in pronunciation, according to the best standards; and, with some satisfaction, would correct an error in either respect by an educated man, which his ear detected at the Bar. He must have read law intensely at some period of his life, for no man of his day knew the doctrines of the common law better.

He came to the Bar in Philadelphia before the adoption of the Constitution of 1776, as his friend,

Edward Tilghman, also did. The books in the office of the Prothonotary of the Supreme Court, of that early day, and in that of the Common Pleas of Philadelphia County, from which Mr. Williams has made his printed Catalogue, cannot be relied on as evidence of *first* admissions to the Bar. The Catalogue records the admission of Edward Tilghman as of March, 1783; whereas his cousin, Chief Justice Tilghman, says, in Lyle v. Richards, that he was in practice at the Bar in 1774, which was immediately after his return from the Temple. Mr. Lewis, by the same Catalogue, was admitted in September Term, 1777, the first Supreme Court which was held by Chief Justice McKean, after his appointment and that of his associates, in July and August, 1777, under the new Constitution, and was put to flight, in the same month, by the entry of the British into the City. There must have been a previous admission, in these instances, by a Colonial Court. Mr. Lewis's name appears as counsel in one of Mr. Dallas's notes, in September, 1778, a case of high treason, and not a very probable position for a gentleman in the first year of his practice; and Mr. Tilghman's appears in a case decided at Nisi Prius in August, 1773, which may be a mistake of a year in the date, or the case may have been concluded in Bank in the following year. During the whole of the Revolution, and for years afterwards, Mr. Lewis was engaged in nearly all the important causes, and especially in cases of high treason, for which he had a special vocation and capacity, and of which there was a plentiful crop in our City of Brotherly Love, up to the advent of peace. "For the divisions of Reuben, there were great searchings of heart," in those days; and the occupation of the City by the enemy, from the close of September, 1777, to the middle of June, 1778, did not heal nor allay them. Perhaps this City was the only judicial school in the country for the law of treason; and it was in this school that Mr. Lewis got his full growth in crown law, and held his high position in it, pretty much without competition, to the close of the century. In treason causes, he was uniformly on the side of the defendant, and was generally successful; and this was the accident that diffused his reputation so far and so widely. He never showed more vigor, self-possession, and dignity, in subsequent periods of his life, than in this description of cause. His deep learning and facility in the law of treason and of other high crimes, was remarkable. He had studied the law of treason, especially, with passion; and had mastered all its details, the law of its process, evidence, and trial, as well as of the offence itself. He knew every vicious excess that had been perpetrated or attempted in furthering the doctrine of constructive treason, for which he felt the utmost abhorrence. He had at the tip of his tongue, all the gibes and scorns that prosecuting attorneys had spit into the faces of the accused, in the oppressive spirit of former times; and would repeat them with disdain at the first symptom of renewal in his presence. I cannot forget the vehemence, amounting to rage, with which, in rebuke of some harsh general reprobation of a prisoner upon trial, he arraigned, as an example to be forever abjured, the Attorney-General Coke, for his brutal language to Sir Walter Raleigh, on the trial of the *bye* and the *main*. "Thou viper! I *thou* thee, thou traitor."—"Thou art thyself a spider of hell."—"Go to, I will lay thee on thy back for the confidentest traitor that ever came to the Bar."

In a letter of the 15th of December, 1778, from President Reed to the father of Jared Ingersoll, afterwards of the Philadelphia Bar, which is published in "The Life and Correspondence of President Reed," by his grandson, there seems to be a pretty broad slur upon the members of this Bar at that epoch: on one part of it as not possessing considerable abilities, and upon the rest as being destitute of political virtue. This, at least, is one of several versions of a clause in the letter. "Our lawyers here," says President Reed, "of any considerable abilities, are all, as I may say, in one interest, and that not the popular one." President Reed was at that time in the popular interest himself, though he had been as much opposed as any one to the Constitution of 1776,—its plural executive and single legislature, and its universal oath of office to do nothing directly or indirectly to prejudice the Constitution and Government, that is to say, not to alter, or to counsel or attempt the altering of, a single feature of it,—until he took office under it himself. On the happening of that event, he led or followed a popular interest, of a certain kind, in the administration of Government. Those times had not yet got into joint; and perhaps the best spirit in which to read the words of the cotemporary actors on every side, is to make the largest abatement from that which is written with the most bitterness and personality. The " popular interest" was undoubtedly, in one sense, the interest of the Confederation, of independence, and of success in the pending conflict. To be false to this, was always a great, and sometimes a just reproach. But there was also a "popular interest," to some extent, in a proscriptive policy, that would leave no man at liberty to counsel moderation or temper, either in social intercourse or in legal regulations, any more than the Constitution of 1776 did to any one of its officers, judicial, civil, or military, in regard to change, or the recommendation of change, in its own stipulations. In the eyes of this "popular interest," every Quaker was a tory or traitor; and all social affinities with that body of men, a body of great respectability, wealth, and order, were regarded as implicating the party in a lesser or greater treason, like the *bye* and the *main* of Sir Walter Raleigh and his friends.

We must read such times with the personal glossary of the writer or speaker at our side, or we shall often fail to understand them. If President Reed meant to describe James Wilson, John Ross, Alexander Wilcocks, William Lewis, Edward Tilghman, and William Bradford, who were all at the Bar in December, 1778, and were undeniably men of "considerable abilities," as being untrue to the Confederation, to independence, or to the success of the country in her struggle, then he wrote from a very partial and prejudiced view. None of these men certainly were of the proscriptive party, nor were they farther from that than from unfaithfulness to the country. Having some knowledge of President Reed's relations in social life, I cannot believe that such was his meaning. I incline to think that he meant no more by it, than that the able part of the Bar was, at that time, on questions of local policy, the losing party at the polls, in which the President was successful. He probably meant no more than to woo his friend's son to his own side in politics, as the best for an opening at the Bar; and as the clause admits of this interpretation, I prefer adopting it. Mr. Lewis was an adherent of the Declaration of Independence, but he was not bitterly proscriptive; and was entitled to much higher praise than that of not refusing his professional aid to those who were hounded by some of the "popular interest," on account of the treason of quiet wishes and preferences for something better than a proscriptive government. He was a republican, and the open and uniform friend of Washington, and of Washington's friends and principles, as were thousands of the best men in Philadelphia, at the side of Mr. Lewis, who, nevertheless, were not, in a certain sense, in the " popular interest."

The prominence of the City of Philadelphia as the seat of the Congress of the Confederation, and her superiority in population and commerce, up to the removal of the seat of the Federal Government to the City of Washington, in 1801, may account, in some degree, for the diffusion of Mr. Lewis's celebrity, which partook of the distinction awarded to the City. But it was not in criminal law alone, that he was deemed, by other cities, to be the most able man at the Bar. He was a person of great intellectual ardor, and of a strong grasp of mind; and both in law and politics, and other matters too, he took firm hold of whatever interested him. His great devotion was, of course, to professional studies. He explored every field of law, common, constitutional, international, commercial, and maritime; and with singular predilection, that very intricate *close* or quarter of the common law, in which the doctrine of pleading is, or formerly was, fenced up from easy access, even against many of the profession. If the fences have been lowered, and in some parts prostrated, in modern times, it may be doubted whether it has not been more for the benefit of estrays, than for the culture of the proper flock, and the good of those who profit by their thorough breeding. The abuse of the doctrine has, at times, been excessive, and is properly restrained or remedied; but the abolition of it, supposing it to be possible, would make a Babel of the court-room. It was Mr. Lewis's notion that nothing but good pleading could prevent a confusion of tongues, upon every important trial; and every sound lawyer is probably of his opinion.

He was much interested in the abolition of slavery within the State of Pennsylvania. Since his death, some questions have been raised in regard to the part, whether active or consultative, that he took in promoting the Act of 1st March, 1780, "for the gradual abolition of slavery in Pennsylvania;" and I do not mean to raise any question of my own. But I am perfectly clear that, in his lifetime, and at the beginning of this century, when others who may now be thought to have been actors in the matter, were living, Mr. Lewis was currently spoken of, at the Bar, as the draughtsman of that Act. Whether the Preamble, as well as the enacting clauses, were said to have come from his pen, I cannot report, because the distinction has first been made since Mr. Lewis's death. Though, in 1779, he was not a lawyer of long standing, he was abundantly mature for the work, and that was the day of young men in the courts and throughout the country. The old men in general, as they always do, and beneficially too, clung to associations of early life, and did not enter freely upon the responsibilities of the new public life that had sprung up around them.

During the two administrations of Washington, and continuously during life, Mr. Lewis was a thorough Federalist, amusingly anti-gallican, and entirely anti-Jeffersonian; and upon law questions of difficulty that arose in the Executive Department, though he was not an official adviser, he was familiarly consulted by General Hamilton, the Secretary of the Treasury, with whom he continued on terms of confidence and mutual respect during General Hamilton's life. The memorable argument of Hamilton, in 1791, upon the constitutionality of the Bank of the United States, or rather of the Bill to incorporate the Subscribers to the Bank, was read to Mr. Lewis before it was sent to the President, as I have heard from Mr. Lewis himself, as well as from one of General Hamilton's sons; but I have never heard a surmise that it was in any respect altered in consequence of this. Its great principles were discussed between the two, sitting in Mr. Lewis's office, or walking in his garden, until all the reasons of the Secretary of the Treasury, and the answers to the objections of the Secretary of State, and of the Attorney-General, were scrupulously examined and weighed. No lawyer could have been better in such a consultation than Mr. Lewis, who was fertile in the suggestion of doubts, and quick in the solution of them, and had an admirable *coup d'œil* to discern the strong and weak points of assault and defence.

That argument of General Hamilton, it should be remembered, first enunciated the great rules of interpretation, by which the powers delegated by the people of the United States to Congress, were to be construed; and they were afterwards tested by the Supreme Tribunal of Federal law, and stood the test then and for sixty years from the adoption of the Constitution. I hope to be excused for thinking that no juridical argument, before or since, has shaken, or ever will shake, those rules of interpretation; and that none other can maintain the constitutional relations of the States and the United States, the one to the other, and give superiority to each in its proper sphere. How much the battle-axe of party may make the lighter scale in some measures the heavier in all, remains for future history. None but a parricidal arm would cast it in; nor can it remain there very long without deranging the orbit of each system, and generating a new centre of gravitation, when both systems may be "folded up as a vesture." If *State rights* mean anything to the contrary of that argument, they mean that the United States shall not be administered by a fair construction of the Constitution, but by the *platforms* of party.

It was a compliment of the first order from the great statesman and constitutional lawyer who elicited the argument, to submit it to the lawyer of Pennsylvania, whom he called into consultation; and Mr. Lewis was justly proud of it, and constantly glorified the man who prostrated, for the time, the political metaphysics of Mr. Jefferson, the first man on his part, also, who broached the doctrine of strict construction against the United States, and of the most liberal, consequently, for the reserved rights of the people and the States. Mr. Jefferson was a true son of Virginia, in his ambition for State supremacy, until he was elected to the Presidency. After that, he surrendered, with modest diffidence, his doctrine of strict construction, to obtain an empire from France. If his friends were satisfied that Louisiana could be brought into the Union without an amendment to the Constitution, he "certainly *would acquiesce with satisfaction;*" "but the less that was said about any constitutional difficulty, the better:" "and it would be desirable for Congress to do what was necessary, *in silence.*" These are his own words. Happy adaptability! Greatest of managers!

Mr. Lewis was always ready to render the like patriotic service to the administration of the Father of his Country; and it was no doubt from this motive, that he accepted the commission of District Judge of the United States for the Pennsylvania District, in the summer of 1791, and held it until the spring of 1792, when Judge Peters was appointed. He must have foregone, for the time, his large professional emoluments, to meet a public exigency on the death of Judge Francis Hopkinson. Mr. Jefferson, in his letter to Mr. Hammond, on the subject of interest on the British debts during the period of the Revolution, cites the opinion of Mr. Lewis in support of his own views; and to meet this question judicially, was perhaps one of his motives for accepting temporarily the appointment.

In February, 1794, he was counsel for the petitioners against the election of Albert Gallatin to the Senate of the United States, by the Legislature of Pennsylvania, and was heard before the Senate: the first occasion on which the Senate opened its doors to professional counsel, or to the public.

The objection to Mr. Gallatin was an alleged defect of citizenship. He was a native of Geneva, in Switzerland. He arrived at Boston, in the United States, in May, 1780; and in October following, he went to reside at Machias, in the District of Maine, where he remained a year, and performed some volunteer military service. He afterwards owned land, and resided in Virginia, and took an oath of allegiance to that State in October, 1785; and supposing this, and not his residence and military service at Machias, to have been the commencement of his citizenship, then he had not been a citizen nine years, which the Constitution requires, when elected. The question has ceased to be of any interest; but it was a great point at that day, when a rising party wanted Mr. Gallatin's financial knowledge and quick eye to point their batteries against the policy of Washington. Mr. Lewis gave himself to the frustration of this object with infinite satisfaction, and succeeded in the Senate by a very slim majority. But substantially it was no success, as Mr. Gallatin was elected to the next House of Representatives.

But it was in the special field of his profession, that Mr. Lewis best exhibited the depth and the purity of his legal learning and principles, and the fine ideal of a great lawyer and advocate by which he was animated. His devotion to the maintenance of the just authority of the Court and jury, and of the rights of the Bar, and of the parties and people, which the study of the common law is so apt to inspire, was not less, than to the repression of any unjust assumption by either of them. In criminal causes especially, whatever powers or prerogatives had been given by Magna Charta, the Constitution, or the law, either to the courts or the people, for the vindication of public justice and order, or for the defence of personal liberty and reputation, had a sleepless guardian in him; and he kindled at nothing sooner than an invasion of any of these great securities, on any side, to the prejudice of either Court or jury, or of the independence of the Bar, or of the full exercise of defence against criminal accusation. In professional life constantly, and in public life when he was called to it, his learning and powers of research, his energy, and his oratory, not seldom rising to the highest order of forensic eloquence, were freely devoted to this his almost ruling passion.

He achieved a great victory at the Bar, and also in the Legislature of Pennsylvania in the year 1788, when a spirit of factious jealousy, under the lead of a very ardent and determined man, aspired to deprive the Supreme Court of the State, of one of its most ancient and necessary powers. As counsel, Mr. Lewis had asserted and maintained the right of the Court to punish Colonel Oswald by fine and imprisonment, without trial by jury, for a contempt of Court, in the columns of a newspaper; and in the Legislature he defeated a very active effort, by some of the strongest members of the Country, to impeach Chief Justice McKean and certain of the Judges for having exercised the power. He did this, though McKean was no friend of his, nor he of McKean. The distinction without a difference, except on the wrong side, as to contempts committed *out of the presence* of the Court, did not then, nor for many years afterwards, prevail; but prevailed finally by positive enactment, rather more perhaps because it was an abridgment of judicial power, the *terriculum* of the democracy, than for any weightier reason; for the most penetrating and corrupting of contempts, such as requires immediate redress, to take an obstruction out of the very path in which a Court of justice is moving at the time, is a contempt *out of Court*, upon the face of a widely diffused newspaper. The laggard redress by indictment is a mere name and a shadow, as ineffectual as a reprieve after execution executed. As far as I know, it has never been resorted to. The impartial trial of a cause which can be made to excite the public interest and passion, is at this time of day hardly possible in Pennsylvania. The Judges must now see in the public press, everything which prejudice or venality may choose to exhibit to their disturbance; and they cannot prevent the jurors from also seeing it. The fillet with which fiction covers the eyes of Justice to make her blind to the inequality of the parties, is taken from her eyes, and her arms are pinioned with it. The old doctrine of contempt of Court, is an immense safeguard to trial by jury.

There was a subsequent occasion, on which Mr. Lewis with much decision asserted the dignity of his profession, and the rights of the defendant and the jury, in opposition to the Court. In this case it was the eloquence of action and not of words.

He had been counsel for John Fries, an insurgent

of Northampton County, in Pennsylvania, upon a former trial before Mr. Justice Iredell, of the Supreme Court of the United States, and Peters the District Judge, upon an indictment for treason, where the law had been fully discussed, and Fries had been convicted. A new trial was awarded by the Court, on the ground of declarations by a juror, ascertained by the defendant and his counsel after the verdict had been rendered. Before a jury was empanelled for the new trial, Mr. Justice Chase, of Maryland, who was in the seat before occupied by Judge Iredell, informed the Bar, that the Court had made up their opinion upon the law of treason involved in the case; and to prevent being misunderstood, they had reduced it to writing, and had directed copies to be made for the District Attorney, the counsel of Fries the prisoner, and the jury; which were then handed for distribution to the Clerk of the Court, who placed them on the table at the Bar. Mr. Lewis with some deliberation and solemnity rose from his seat, slowly approached the papers, and lifting one of them to his eyes, gave a short glance at it, and threw it down upon the table. He then withdrew, and retired from the place he had occupied, without uttering a word. Mr. Edward Tilghman approached him, said a few words to him about the innovation, and after the transaction of some other business, the Court adjourned for the day. On the next morning, when the cause was called, Mr. Lewis informed the Court, that upon full and solemn consideration, he declined proceeding as counsel for the prisoner, as the Court had prejudged the law; and Mr. Dallas his colleague, declared himself to the same effect, though with a hesitation, he said, which he would not have felt, if the Court had not appointed him as assistant counsel for the prisoner. There was profound silence, and deep sensation at the Bar, and the Court had no doubt been previously led to expect it; for Judge Chase informed the counsel, that they were not bound by the opinion, but might contest it on both sides, and Judge Peters expressed a *wish* that the counsel would proceed, and take the course they should think proper. The papers, he said, were withdrawn. The Judge had probably deferred to Judge Chase, and let the papers go as the opinion of the Court, without any very cordial sanction. Mr. Lewis, with few, but distinct and solemn words, replied: " The Court has prejudged the law of the case—the opinion of the Court has been declared—after such a declaration, the counsel can have no hope of changing it,—the impression of it must remain with the jury,—the counsel, therefore, will not act in behalf of the prisoner." The effect was electric; for Mr. Lewis had the full sympathy of the Bar.

Judge Chase, however, did not forget his personal dignity, nor the dignity of the Bench, upon hearing this definitive reply. He immediately rejoined to the effect, that then, with God's help, the Court would be the counsel of the prisoner, and would see that he had a fair trial. And no doubt he had a fair trial, and was convicted a second time, and sentenced to death. But the pardon that ensued was not improbably induced, in part, by what had happened. The life of the prisoner was saved, and the conduct of Judge Chase was made an article of the impeachment subsequently preferred against him by the House of Representatives; and sixteen out of thirty-four senators recorded against him, upon that charge, the vote of guilty. The larger number voted for his acquittal, upon the ground, probably, of the absence of all corrupt or oppressive intention. It was acknowledged that the previously declared opinion of the Court had been sound in point of law.

I was present at this scene, in April, 1800, and have given it as my memory retains it. The act of the Court was not regarded by the Bar as one of intended oppression of either the prisoner or his counsel, but as a great mistake, resulting, in part, from the character of the principal judge, a very learned and able man, but confident and rather imperious, and in part from his greater familiarity with the Maryland practice, where the Judge used to respond, and perhaps still does, more exclusively for the law, and the jury for the facts, or rather more dividedly or separately, than was, in point of form, the usage in Pennsylvania. In a criminal cause like this, however, the course of the Court would probably have been regarded as a mistake anywhere. It served as a signal lesson to stimulate the sense of professional independence, in asserting all the rights of counsel, of the accused, and of the jury, in criminal causes; and fitly closed Mr. Lewis's career in this description of case.

The range of judicial questions which occurred between the peace of 1783, with Great Britain, and the end of the last Federal Administration of the Government, in the year 1801, the most brilliant part of Mr. Lewis's professional life, and when his intellectual powers were certainly in their zenith, was remarkably large and important. Before the country had attained the lawful age of man or woman, the fullest demands for juridical wisdom and experience were upon it. Questions of prize and of the jurisdiction of the admiralty, — questions concerning the rights of ambassadors and the privileges of consuls,— concerning the obligations of neutrality, the right of expatriation, the right of naturalization by the States, the construction of the treaty of peace with Great Britain, the case of the Virginia debts, and of confiscations and attainders complete or incomplete before the peace, the constitutional powers of the Federal Courts, the powers of Congress, the constitutionality of the carriage tax, the nature and characteristics of direct taxes imposed under the Federal Constitution,

—questions of conflict between the authority of the States and of the United States, and between the States severally under the Confederation, and cases of high crimes, both at sea and on land, against the United States, were rising up from day to day for solution; and in most of them Mr. Lewis took a part, and held a position, that was worthy of the questions, and worthy of his own powers also.

His general manner in arguing an important cause, cannot be well appreciated by the reader, without some recollection of his rather peculiar person and countenance; and yet the effect of the whole man in action, was so remote or different from the appearance of his person at rest, that no one could infer the one from the other. At rest, strictly speaking, he never was, while in Court; but when he was not trying or arguing a cause, he was quizzing or joking, or mooting or smoking, generally in a state of unrest. When fully engaged in argument, he saw nothing and thought of nothing but his cause; and, in that, would sometimes rise to the fervor and energy of a sibyl.

He was about six feet in height as he stood, and would have been more if he had been bent back to a perpendicular from the curve,—not a stoop of the shoulders,—in which he habitually inclined forwards. At the same time he was very spare of flesh, and destitute of almost all dimensions but length.

His countenance was intellectual, but its general

effect was hurt by his spectacles, and by the altitude and length of his nose, of which, nevertheless, he was immensely proud. The nose so entirely absorbed the expression of his eyes and the rest of his features, that most of the young gentlemen at the Bar, in his time, could draw a striking likeness of Mr. Lewis, by a simple outline of his nose. When the spectacles were entirely removed from his eyes, to see or read near at hand, you perceived that their expression was kindly and gentle; but when he looked through his glasses at the Court or jury, they assumed the expression that belonged to the sentiment or passion that moved him, and sometimes it was a rather truculent one.

He abominated the Gallican invention, as he called it, of pantaloons, and stuck to knee breeches all his life; and, under the same prejudice, he adhered to hair powder and a cue, because the French revolutionists had first rejected them from their armies. When he presented himself, in what he deemed the only forensic dress, a full suit of black and powdered head, even a stranger would expect to hear something worth hearing from that animated and imposing figure; and by the first sentences of his speech, usually addressed, with a self-confident sweep of the head, and in a deep baritone voice, to the Court, and, if necessary, to the jury, the attention of every one would be arrested.

His first attitude was always as erect as he could make it, with one hand insinuated between his waistcoat and his shirt, and the other lying loose upon his loin; and in this position, without any action but that movement of the head, he would utter two or three of his first sentences, generally well-prepared to introduce some notice of the position and solicitude of his client, or some special characteristic of the case, and almost universally, some general principle or truth that he held to underlie his client's cause, and to bespeak the favor of the Court and jury. Then, with a quick movement, and sometimes with a little jerk of the body, he would bring both his hands to his sides, and begin the action. And it was pretty vehement action from that time to the conclusion; his head dropping or rising, his body bending or straightening up, and his arms singly or together relieving his head, and doing their part of a rather animated duty, but without a vestige of grace or preparation in any of his movements, all of them, however, sympathizing with the temper or expression of the moment. His voice never failed him. It was deep, sonorous, and clear to the last; and his pronunciation, without the least monotony or affectation, always conformed to the best standards in the language.

He had one, and I think only one, peculiarity, which never deserted him in solemn speaking, though it was not observable in conversation. It was not, strictly speaking, an accent, nor a pronunciation, but rather had the air of an impediment,—a lingering upon a few unemphatic words, as if he could not get them out. It was no impediment, however; but he dwelt upon them with the purpose of making them more emphatic. *Clear* and *plain* were two of these words. He was sometimes faulty in his taste, even in a grave harangue; and one of the recollections of this which remains the most distinctly with me, reminds me of this peculiarity, and at the same time of his sleepless anti-gallicanism.

He was arguing a very grave cause in the Supreme Court of the United States on a morning which had brought the news of some fresh atrocity in the French Revolution; and, after laying down a position of law, and proving or defending it with great strength and skill, having no relation however to France, or to the Revolution, or to anything associated with either, he exclaimed, "And this, may it please your Honors, is as cul-lear and as pul-lain as that the Devil is in Paris, and *that* nobody can doubt." Plain was always *pul-lain*, and clear *cul-lear*, in Mr. Lewis's solemn arguments. There were two or three other words of one syllable, with an *l* as the turning letter, that he clung to in the same manner in his harangues.

It may be perceived, from this account of him, that Mr. Lewis never dozed in his speeches, nor let any one else doze, who was within hearing. Yet he was never vociferous. His voice was not sweet, but it was a fine working voice for a court-room. He was animated, sonorous, and continuous or sustained to the end, without break or pause, except to lift his spectacles, and cast his eye upon his sheet of notes; and he brought all his arguments to a close within a reasonable compass of time.

It would be regarded by every one who knew him, as a defect in this description of Mr. Lewis, if two or three of his *maculæ*, perhaps *nebulæ*, were painted out, or left without notice, since he was as well known by them as by his better parts, and he took as little pains to cover them up. The spots or clouds were in the outward man, and the deepest of them not so deep perhaps as he inclined to have it thought. They did not touch his professional integrity, nor his fidelity to the law.

He smoked cigars incessantly. He smoked at the fireplace in Court. He smoked in the Court Library. He smoked in his office. He smoked in the street. He smoked in bed; and he would have smoked in church, like Knockdunder, in the Heart of Mid Lothian, if he had ever gone there. The servitude was unremitting, as to a most imperious master. It did not look like an accommodation to health or to taste, but like submission to a conquest by external power.

The smoking in bed was, in one instance, literally verified by myself and my venerable master, upon a winter journey to the Supreme Court at Washington, in the year 1809, when, in the days of coaching, we passed our first night at the Head of Elk; and I called Mr. Ingersoll's attention to it, after we had got into our respective beds in the same large room, and the last candle had been extinguished. The cigar was then seen firing up from Mr. Lewis's pillow, and disappearing in darkness, like a revolving light on the coast. He was once ordered into the custody of the Marshal, by Judge Chase, who affected to believe that the audacity was in some interloper at the chimney corner of the court-room; but Judge Peters explained, *sotto voce*, and it passed. The cigar did not reappear in that presence. In the Supreme Court of the State it was winked at before the time of Chief Justice Tilghman; but soon after he came to the Bench, it was relegated to the Library. It had been tolerated the longer because no one imitated the example, and it had the asserted apology of weak health.

Mr. Lewis sometimes exhibited a stain of an antecedent day, in indelicate allusions at the side Bar, and in the presence of younger men, as well as of his cotemporaries, with all of whom he did not seem to be unwilling to have it pass, that he led a careless, convivial, and half-libertine life, much beyond the reality. This, however, was while he was a widower, having no young children about him, and before his second marriage to a most pleasing lady who survived him. The influence of the sex, as much perhaps as better moral perceptions and taste, has, in later times, expelled such *opprobria* from the presence of gentlemen, everywhere.

But the spots most annoying to the Bar, were discernible in his practice there, in the later years of his life, without, however, committing his professional honor, or bringing any serious inconvenience upon his clients. They were, it is true, not constantly seen, but still not unfrequently. He was singularly chary of his reputation for skill and efficiency in the trial of causes; and if he was not well prepared at the necessary moment, as sometimes happened when he grew older, he would baffle the Bench and the Bar in their efforts to bring him into action. In such an emergency he would show a great fertility of device in eluding the trial or argument for the time, and when every other failed, he would be inimitably indisposed in health. His great resort, if compelled to go on, and he had the conclusion of the argument, was to study his cause while it was in progress before the Court, as he could do, intensely, and bring out new points, after his adversaries had closed upon all that had been advanced in the opening. The Court was compelled to meet this practice by a general rule prohibiting new points by the concluding counsel. The rule was general, but the aim of it was exclusively directed at Mr. Lewis. He was never uncandid, except from some such necessity,—which a better use of that part of his time, which belonged to his clients, would have obviated. There seemed to be no native taint in him; his heart was kind and true, his principles in general were manly, and his friendships sincere and constant. He looked upon this practice, unfortunately, I think, as a license of professional strategy in the service of his clients. A little less confidence in his intellectual powers, and a little more prudence in the economy of time, would have saved him from a distrust on such occasions by the older men of the Bar, which might sometimes be seen when they were opposed to him in the trial of a cause.

These were spots in the sun, you may say; but from the time I first knew him they were observable and observed; so much so, that to have omitted all notice of them, would have impaired the truth of the description, personal and professional, that I have endeavored to give of him.

The last cause he tried was Willing v. Tilghman, in the spring of 1819; where, on behalf of the late Chief Justice, the defendant, I opposed him. I well remember that the Chief Justice, who had been his cotemporary at the Bar, and who was urgent for the trial, expected that I should have to meet Mr. Lewis's now very usual effort for procrastination, and stood near me to affirm my opposition, until the jury was sworn, when he retired from the court-room. In the course of Mr. Lewis's reply, he became faint, and sat down, but soon recovered himself and went on. On this occasion his indisposition was certainly unfeigned. He never appeared in Court afterwards, and died in the month of August following.

There can be no doubt whatever that Mr. Lewis was a very learned lawyer, fully awake to the elevation and dignity of his profession, and prompt to maintain them whenever vindication was necessary, though occasionally unbending a little too much at the side Bar. He was a clear and logical reasoner, and of very vigorous mind, rising at times, in his oral arguments, to the highest eloquence of reason, though no man cultivated less the graces of oratory. He was moreover subtle, ingenious, full of resources, and perhaps as shining an advocate in a bad or doubtful cause, as he was able in a good one. In some points he was not without resemblance to *Saunders*, his favorite authority, in both the strength and weakness of his parts—something less strong perhaps, and decidedly less weak. He contributed much to elevate the standard of law and of professional effort at the Bar; and if he had possessed a little more *retenue*, might have done as much for the standard of manners, wherein he fell something short; less however in reality, than by contrast with the high professional carriage of his eminent cotemporaries.

EDWARD TILGHMAN.

EDWARD TILGHMAN.

I PLACE in advance of some remarks of the present day, a short sketch of this admirable lawyer, written a few years since for a work which was published in Philadelphia.

"TILGHMAN (Edward); an eminent lawyer of the State of Pennsylvania, at the Bar of Philadelphia. He was born at Wye, on the Eastern Shore of Maryland, on the 11th of December, 1750, of an old and respectable family, which in the paternal line emigrated to the province of Maryland from Kent County in England, about the year 1662. His academical education was received in the City of Philadelphia, under teachers who were successful in accomplishing him in the ancient classics, to an extent which, at a subsequent time, now happily passed away, it was the poor fashion to undervalue or decry. His education in the law was obtained principally in the Middle Temple, of which he was entered a student about the year 1771; and in the years 1772 and 1773 he became an assiduous attendant upon the Courts of Westminster Hall, taking notes of the arguments in Chancery before Lord Apsley, and of such men as Wallace, Dunning, Davenport, and Mansfield, before Lord Mansfield and the Judges of the King's Bench. His note-books are still extant in the possession of his descendants; and one of them was of remarkable use upon the argument of Clayton against Clayton, in the Supreme Court of Pennsylvania, in explaining an obscure report by Sir James Burrow, of Lord Mansfield's judgment in Wigfall v. Brydon, which was cited before the same Judges in Goodright v. Patch, in 1773, and then put upon its true ground. After finishing his course at the Middle Temple, he returned to Philadelphia, and was admitted to the Bar, at which he continued till his death, on the 1st of November, 1815, in the sixty-fifth year of his age.

"There are two very different methods of acquiring a knowledge of the law of England, and by each of them men have succeeded in public estimation to an almost equal extent. One of them, which may be called the old way, is a methodical study of the general system of law, and of its grounds and reasons, beginning with the fundamental law of estates and tenures, and pursuing the derivative branches in logical succession, and the collateral subjects in due order, by which the student acquires a knowledge of principles that rule in all departments of the science, and learns to feel, as much as to know, what is in harmony with the system, and what is not. The other is to get an outline of the system by the aid of commentaries, and to fill it up by the desultory reading of treatises and reports, according to the bent of the student, without much shape or certainty in the knowledge so acquired, until it is given by investigations in the course of practice. A good deal of law may be put together by a facile or flexible man in the second of these modes, and the public are often satisfied with it; but the profession itself knows the first, by its fruits, to be the most effectual way of making a great lawyer. Edward Tilghman took the old way, and acquired in it not only great learning, but the most accurate legal judgment of any man of his day, at the Bar of which he was a member. No one of his cotemporaries would have felt injured by his receiving this praise. Upon questions which to most men are perplexing at first, and continue to be so until they have worked their way to a conclusion by elaborate reasoning, he seemed to possess an instinct, which seized the true result before he had taken time to prove it. This was no doubt the fruit of severe and regular training, by which his mind became so imbued with legal principles, that they unconsciously governed his first impressions. In that branch of the law which demands the greatest subtlety of intellect, as well as familiarity with principles, the chapter of contingent remainders and executory devises, he had probably no superior anywhere. An eminent Judge has said of him, 'that he never knew any man who had this branch of the law so much at his finger ends. With all others with whom he had had professional intercourse, it was the work of time and consideration to comprehend; but he took in with one glance all the beauties of the most obscure and difficult limitations. With him it was intuitive, and he could untie the knots of a contingent remainder or executory devise as familiarly as he could his garter.' When this can be justly said of a lawyer—and it was said most justly of Edward Tilghman—nothing is wanting to convey to professional readers an adequate notion of the extent of his learning, and the grasp of his understanding; for the doctrines upon these subjects are the higher mathematics of the law, and the attainment of them by any one, implies that the whole domain lies at his feet. Mr. Tilghman was also an advocate of great powers —a master of every question in his causes—a wary tactician in the management of them—highly accomplished in language—a faultless logician—a man of the purest integrity and of the brightest honor—fluent without the least volubility—concise to a degree that left every one's patience and attention unimpaired— and perspicuous to almost the lowest order of understandings, while he was dealing with almost the highest topics. How could such qualities as these fail to give him a ready acceptance with both courts and juries, and to make him the bulwark of any cause which his judgment approved? An invincible aversion to authorship and to public office, has prevented this great lawyer from being known as he ought to have been, beyond the limits of his own country. He has probably left nothing professional behind him but his opinions upon cases, now in various hands, and difficult to collect, but which, if collected and published, would place him upon the same elevation with Dulany, of Maryland, or Fearne, the author of the work in which he most delighted. The Chief Justiceship of the Supreme Court of Pennsylvania was offered to him by Governor McKean, upon the death of Chief Justice Shippen; but he declined it, and recommended for the appointment his kinsman, William Tilghman, who so much adorned that station by his learning and virtues.

"It is instructive to record, that the stern acquirements and labors of this eminent man never displaced the smiles of benevolence from his countenance, nor put the least weight upon his ever buoyant spirit. His wit was as playful and harmless, and almost as bright, as heat lightning upon a summer's evening. It always lit up the edges of the clouds of controversy that surrounded the Bar, and sometimes dispersed the darkest and angriest. A more frank, honorable, and gentlemanly practitioner of the law, and one more kind, communicative, and condescending to the young students and members of the Bar, never lived. The writer of this article, thirty years his junior, regards it as his greatest good fortune to have been admitted to the familiar intimacy of Edward Tilghman, and to have enjoyed not only instruction from his learning and wisdom, but an example of life in his cheerfulness and serenity, during the vicissitudes of health and fortune which chequered his declining years."

The preceding article was written by request of a daughter of Edward Tilghman, for the supplementary volume of the Encyclopædia Americana, edited by Professor Vethake, now Provost of the University of Pennsylvania. As it has been reprinted more than once in the public journals, I do not break it up into a rather fuller sketch of its eminent subject, but leave it unaltered, as a condensed account of Mr. Tilghman's parentage and education, and of his profound attainments in the deep-sea learning of the law, far off from common soundings, as well as of his pleasant wit and most benign temper. But it may be useful to give a little further extension and detail to the subject, by some particulars of his education in the law, and of his professional and personal character. A notice of them in the article, would have extended it too much for the work in which it was published, and perhaps would have imparted to it either a too professional or a too familiar air. These particulars are as fresh with me now as when I first knew them, some of them sixty years ago, and will not be, I think, without interest to such of the members of the Bar as recollect him or have heard much of him.

Of the perfect confidence of the Judges in his opinions, I will refer to two or three instances in this place, without, at present, including an obituary notice immediately after his death, which will be allowed to be authoritative when I shall name its author.

In the well-argued and important case of Finlay's Lessee v. Riddle, reported in 3 Binney, 139, the question of law was one of those which are sometimes called *gordian*. It was a devise of an estate to A. for his natural life, and after his decease, if he shall die leaving lawful issue, to his *heirs* as tenants in common, and their respective heirs and assigns forever; but in case he shall die without leaving lawful issue, then to B., his brother, to hold to him and his heirs and assigns forever. Of course, "the pinch of the case," as Judge Brackenridge called it, was in the word *heirs*, as first used, whether it was to be regarded as a word of limitation, or as a word of purchase; that is to say, whether A. took an estate tail, or an estate for life only. Chief Justice Tilghman, before whom the cause was tried at a Circuit Court, told the jury that the inclination of his mind was rather in favor of the opinion that A. took only an estate for life; but as it was a question of considerable difficulty, he would reserve the point; and he directed the jury to find a verdict in correspondence with his inclination. Of the same opinion were all the Judges finally. Judge Brackenridge, in giving his opinion, said, " that something was thrown out in the course of the argument at the Bar, by the counsel contending for the estate tail,"—the same gentleman who afterwards, as a Judge of the same Court, so distinctly affirmed the supremacy of Edward Tilghman in this branch of the law, —" of a confidence in what the opinion would be, of the elder of the profession, were it taken on this devise. The case being held under advisement, and it so happening that I had an easy opportunity, I put the case to one of the eldest and ablest of the profession in the State, and totally unconcerned in the matter, but submitted merely as a problem in legal science, in that abstruse part of it, the doctrine of devises and contingent remainders. His note to me I hold in my hands, and will read it." And then follows, in the printed report, without the author's name, a page of short, close, pithy sentences, after the writer's fashion, affirming the estate for life only, and unloosing the knot " familiar as his garter." The writer of that note was Edward Tilghman.

Another instance of the respect entertained for him by the foremost Judge on the Bench, occurred in my presence. It was a case in which Chief Justice Tilghman did not concur with the argument of his cousin, and put to him two or three objections, which were answered, and the argument then was pressed in its first direction. At the close, the Chief Justice said, "Mr. Tilghman, I have so much respect for your judgment, and so much knowledge of your sincerity in what you press, that I will look further into the point."

A third occurred in the great case of the Bush Hill estate, Lyle v. Richards, 9 Serg. & Rawle, which grew out of a common recovery, that I had conducted with his support and advice. It was in this case that Judge Duncan, after Mr. Tilghman's death, pronounced the eulogy upon him that is mentioned in the article.

In that emphatic praise, Judge Duncan said of him, "that, with one glance, he took in all the beauties of the most obscure and difficult limitations. With him it was intuition." And this was so far true, that it had that appearance. But Mr. Tilghman's intuition, in such cases, took in more than is included in the letter of Mr. Locke's definition. It was not only the immediate perception of the agreement or disagreement of two ideas in the party's own mind, but the immediate grouping of reasons and authorities, and the unconscious comparison of them, and the giving out the true result in a moment, as it happens with an accomplished performer on the organ, who expresses a whole score without consciously perusing the parts of it. This was, in reality, deduction so infinitely quick, that it had the appearance of intuition.

It was this quick and accurate glance that distinguished him in his arguments at the Bar. The difference between cases which to some men appeared contradictory or discordant,—the little more or the little less in circumstance,—he knew, and could touch as quickly as a musician touches the flats and sharps of the key-board; and he did it without the least affectation of learning, passing along them, from one key to another, with the purest modulation, and bringing them into harmony with the key of his own argument.

No man talked less at the Bar for talk's sake, or less frequently resorted to words for want of thoughts. His plain and direct reasoning was very rarely embellished by anything that was collateral. He kept the narrow and straight way, and culled little or nothing from the fields alongside; yet he intermixed the reasons of the law with its principles, so smoothly and shrewdly, that he never was dry or abstruse. When he began, he generally meant to say all that he afterwards said, rarely or never leaving his path; and when his argument was at an end, he did not utter a word to round it off,—no peroration, no retouching, no supplemental answers to objections,—all had been noticed and disposed of in due order as he advanced.

In no instance did he argue a cause superficially, nor in any did his cousin, Chief Justice Tilghman, decide a cause *hastily*. The characteristics of both, as to preparation, deliberation, and caution, were the same. The case of Newlin v. Newlin, 1 Sergeant & Rawle, which asserted the right of a married woman to dispose of her separate trust estate, unless restrained by the deed of trust, was argued by Edward Tilghman and John Sergeant, and was decided in Bank, after mature consideration, by Chief Justice Tilghman and Yeates, who delivered full opinions, affirming the right. The case of Dolan v. Lancaster, 1 Rawle, in the time of Chief Justice Gibson, overruled Newlin v. Newlin, and swept away every vestige of authority from a married woman, during coverture, to alienate or pledge her separate trust estate. Chief Justice Gibson said, that "Newlin v. Newlin was *hastily* determined upon an exception to evidence." He never made a greater mistake, unless when he overruled the authority. It was argued upon pre-existing authorities, which are cited in the report, and came before the Court upon a writ of error to the Common Pleas. It has taken more than one Act of Assembly to patch the hole in the law that was made by Dolan v. Lancaster; and it is not well patched yet. Chief Justice Gibson has delivered good opinions; but he never was less sure-footed than when the shadow of his predecessor fell upon his path.

Imagine the terror of the old authorities at the flash of his cimiter in Ferree v. The Commonwealth, 8 Serg. & Rawle: "For myself, I shall never consent to give effect to a claim by the husband, or those in his stead, to what was at any time the wife's real estate, where it is possible to defeat it by any construction, however forced!" Where is the limit to the possibilities of forced construction? Where is the wisdom of a crotchet, that would tie the hands of all womankind, because a few of them are thought not to have wills of their own?

With a certain description of juries, and by similar intuition of all that bore upon his case, Edward Tilghman was nearly irresistible. He talked to the panel as if he was one of them; as if he was opening to his brethren the path in which they had to walk with him in the discharge of a duty, that was a duty of conscience equally to them and to himself. This of course implies that he knew his jury would understand him, and that he thought his case would bear any quantity of sifting. If he thought either the jury or his cause in fault, he threw nothing away upon either, and reserved himself for a better occasion. But, at all times, his sense and shrewdness, occasional pleasantry, and constant air of sincerity, made it delightful to listen to him. He never condescended to propitiate a dishonest prejudice, rarely a prejudice of any kind. He would laugh at it, and sometimes give it a touch of the whip; but he never coaxed it or wheedled it, or set up a counter prejudice to contend with it. Some of this may at times be proper, but it was not his way. If he thought his cause a good one, and the tribunal an intelligent one, he walked to victory with the most easy and assured step possible. In such a case, before Judge Washington, I heard him once say at the conclusion of his argument, when a colleague was to follow him, "I have now finished what I had to say in the case, and I will let my colleague lose it if he can;" and this he said without the least vanity or triumph, but as if he was merely giving a voice to what others had thought before he was done.

But we must not infer, from this account of him, that the knowledge of remainders and executory devises, came to him, or comes to any man, by inspiration. He worked hard for what he knew, and began early. I have read those note-books, recording his attendance in Westminster Hall, from 1772 to the beginning of 1774; and there, at his age of twenty-two, I have seen, as any one may, the seeds and plants which grew up into that marvellous intuition. The books are in the form of receipt books, with clasps at the end, of a size to be easily carried in the hand, Law being recorded at one end, and Equity at the other; and are full, it would seem, of all the cases of importance which had been argued in his time. They note the points or questions—the name of the counsel who argued—a summary of their arguments and authorities—the dicta of the Judges, and the opinion of the Court, sometimes abbreviated almost into short hand, half a word, and frequently the initial and final letters being made to stand for a word, connectives being omitted where they could be implied; and there is, in some instances, an authority or a remark of his own, interlined, showing that he had taken the notes in Court, perhaps on his knee, and had conned them over in private, especially such as involved great principles, like Goodright v. Patch, where Lord Mansfield explained his opinion in Wigfall v. Bryden, and perhaps damaged that case a little, and in Doe v. Burville, a case of cross-remainders, Campbell v. Power, and other cases, bearing on Mr. Tilghman's favorite subject. His accuracy of language, and perspicuity, are remarkable throughout. In one case, Morgan v. Jones, he says: " Upon what legal grounds Lord Mansfield founded his opinion, in what particular way he effectuated the intention, and according to what rules, I could not understand, being in a crowd and at a distance. However, this I heard him say plainly: ' 'Tis now settled that marriage and having children is a revocation of a will of land.' " His constancy in attending the arguments and judgments in the several Courts—for his note-books report the cases in the King's Bench, Common Pleas, High Court of Chancery, and, in a few instances, the sittings before

Lord Mansfield—is remarkable; and the precision of his abbreviated words, in noticing what fell from counsel or Court, much of which was technical and abstruse, was striking, at his age, and shows him to have been not only a vigilant, but a most intelligent, student; and, as he followed his profession with ardor, it is not difficult to understand the cause of that "intuition" of which Judge Duncan spoke. There was so much in his own mind to behold, and he had looked upon it so frequently and habitually, in at least the great department of estates and tenures, that his quickness and certainty were like those of the eye when it takes in a landscape or a picture.

Besides the labor and attention which his note-books imply, they also bear frequent traces of the same pleasant sparkle which so often twinkled like a star in the face of our own Bar and Court.

It is probable that Lord Mansfield maintained great dignity on the Bench, and delivered himself with some formality and elegance, more, on occasions, than the juniors thought necessary. One of the note-books has this note: "1773, May 21. Lord Mansfield. 'I will not give judgment to-day, but on Monday.' N.B. Lord Mansfield said this with usual perspicuity and emphasis."

Again. "King's Bench. Thursday, 7 Feb. 1774. Campbell v. Hall, Esquire. Special verdict. *Lord Mansfield.* 'What a farrago Sir John gave us yesterday!'—meaning Sir John Dalrymple, in the matter of

Literary Property. *Sir Richard Aston.* 'Strange stuff! His criticism upon "no longer" was against him.' *Lord Mansfield.* 'Sad stuff, Sir Richard! This will prove sad stuff.'"

Again. In this instance the words are given with Mr. Tilghman's abbreviations:

" Indt. sp. conts. wds. of J. of P. in Ex. of Off. Objt. not suff'y certain. Rex v. Barr."

"*Burland.* 'Where only one time in Indt. v. and a. must rel. to that. Adt. and ibid. verbt. in Indt. stds. for both stroke and asst. Hawks. Hale.'"

"——, ad idem. Indt. is that —— was a Justice on 6th June, and that a petty sess'n was held before him and an'r, and deft. then and there spoke the words, ' you don't do justice.' "

"*Serg. Davy.* ' I wont trouble your Lds. with a wd. from Hale or Sergt. Hawkins, but I believe a word or two from Sergt. Davy will do. Indt. is, —— was a Justice before 6th June, and ever since has been. Ergo, if then and there refers to the 6th June, he must have spoke the words " before and ever since." '

" *Ld. M.* ' 'Tis a flat objection.' "

A Mr. Morgan, a barrister of that day, is well known to have acquired the *sobriquet* of *Frog* Morgan, from his manner of citing Cro. Eliz., Cro. Jac., Cro. Car., as *Croak* Elizabeth, &c., and not *Crook*. His voice probably assisted to nick the name. Mr. Tilghman never omits to give him a fling.

One of the note-books records: "Mr. Morgan, with much solemnity, moved for an information against a constable for refusing to run after a person against whom he had a warrant, when that person ran away; and for jeering and deriding the Overseers of the Poor, who obtained the warrant."

"*Sir Richard Aston.* 'The constable ought to have run; but it is not a fit subject for an information. Indict him.' So Frog took nothing by his motion."

In another case—Lord Sandwich against Miller, a motion to change the venue—after noting the argument of Serjeant Glyn, contra, the note proceeds, "Morgan, n. b. Frog, ad idem."

A triplet on the first page of the note-book, runs thus:—

> "My prayer grant, ye Gods, and your altars shall smoke,
> That as he goes home, Frog's neck may be broke,
> And then we shall never more hear the whelp *croak.*"

The temper of this profound lawyer was as remarkable as his learning. His pleasantry made a luminous circle around him whenever he was in a cluster of his friends; and it was particularly bright when two or three of them accompanied him in a walk for recreation. On such occasions, quotations from English or Latin poetry, in aid of his pleasantry, were frequent and pointed: but he was neither a jester nor a satirist. His wit seemed to escape from him, its flow was so easy and lambent, and it neither raised a blister nor left a sting in any one. A friend, who could appreciate his wit, called at his office to pay his *honorarium*. "I am come, Mr. Tilghman, to pay you for winning my cause, which delights me;" and then pulling a purse of gold from his pocket, and taking some broad pieces from it,—"Come, hold out your hand,—one, two, three, four,—tell me when to stop,"—Mr. Tilghman looked at him with his bright smile, and replied,

"Lay on, Macduff,
And damned be him that first cries, hold—enough!"

The world seems to be of opinion that this might be a motto for the Barrister's Arms; but it would hardly be a sufficient distinction.

His friends were rather a select body, and it was with them that this airy temper was freest. Those with whom he was most intimate, derived from his unreserve the same sort of compliment to themselves that Cotton did from Izaak Walton's keeping company with him. "For my father Walton," says Cotton, "will be seen twice in no man's company that he does not like, and likes none but such as he believes to be very honest men, which is one of the best arguments, or at least of the best testimonies, that I either am, or that he thinks me one of those, seeing that I have not yet found him weary of me." It is thought, however, that old Izaak overvalued a little the morality of his adopted son.

Mr. Tilghman's heart, moreover, was as true as his temper. No one was less demonstrative, or made fewer professions, but he held to those he loved with hooks of steel; and if these were ruptured, the wrench seemed to give his heart the greater susceptibility.

There was the utmost simplicity in his dress, and in his address and manners. Though no man was less a Quaker, no man less affected decorative forms of any kind. He never wore black, that I recollect, at the Bar, nor hair powder, though everybody else wore it; nor appeared to give a thought to his outward appearance, though he was always perfectly well kept. He was rather of short stature, spare of flesh, and of delicate but well-proportioned frame. His complexion was fair, and his brown hair was without a thread of gray in it to the last. His face was oval, his nose slightly aquiline, and the shape of his forehead and chin corresponded with this outline. But his eyes and his mouth were his most expressive features; his mouth even more than his eyes. Whatever was the thought that was to come from him, grave or gay, the motion of his lips, before he spoke, was the harbinger of its character. Indeed, it was not difficult to tell what reception he gave to an argument he was listening to, by the opening and shutting of those flexible and mobile valves. When a little pinched, you might easily discover it, by his chewing one of them, until he had cleared away the difficulty. But over all his countenance, and over all his acts, in Court or out of Court, a kind and intelligent nature had diffused the expression of truth, wisdom, and sincerity. There are very few now living, at the Bar, who have any remembrance of his person, and I have therefore given this detail.

In August, 1798, a person, most respectably connected, who was a neighbor of Mr. Tilghman's, and in the kindest relations with him, as he was with many, committed a number of forgeries, which became known, simultaneously, after the banks had closed for the day, and drove him to immediate concealment and flight. I recollect well the deep resentment of the City. This individual had abused Mr. Tilghman's confidence, and had injured him in point of fortune; and no one heard, at that time or afterwards, anything to palliate the crime he had committed. I may add that he was never permitted to return to his family, but died in exile from Pennsylvania; not, however, without having given proofs of repentance, by efforts in a humble way, to do good to the poor and to the sick, as far as his limited supply from others permitted.

In the night that followed the discovery, when he was about to fly, Mr. Tilghman, knowing that he must depart in poverty and wretchedness, took a large purse of gold in his hands, and went to his place of concealment. The only words he spoke to the flying man, when he entered his room, were these: "———, I laid up this for a rainy day; but as I do not believe that any trouble can fall on me or mine, as bitter as yours, take it, and may it do you good. Farewell!"

Yet trouble did fall upon him, without his fault, and of unutterable bitterness too; and he bore it with a fortitude and resignation in which no martyr could have surpassed him. He let concealment feed upon his fortune, and upon his health, that he might keep pain from those he loved. The sacrifice may have been a misjudgment on his part. There were some who thought it was; but it would have been a bold word to express to one, whose judgment for everybody else was the best in the world. I knew him and saw him in the agony of that day, and reverenced him for the heroism of the fortitude with which he parted with nearly all his active property, put down his carriage, and sold his long-accustomed habitation, that his determination might be accomplished without possibility of failure. In the last walk of any length that he took, from the City to his farm in Delaware County, about eighteen months before his death, I was his only companion; and while crossing the last field to his house, he stopped at a fence, and told me that two days before he had accomplished the full sacrifice. The only comment that he made was, "I am sorry that my good wife must, for the rest of her days, go afoot."

Mrs. Tilghman was a daughter of Benjamin Chew, a Chief Justice of the Supreme Court of Pennsylvania before the Revolution, and afterwards President of the High Court of Errors and Appeals. Up to the time of her husband's death, she was for many years in infirm health, and sometimes suffered almost the extremity of pain and illness, becoming the cause of constant solicitude to him; but she survived him twenty-six years, for several of them with improving health, the compensation perhaps of some of the luxuries she had been compelled to forego; and at length died at the venerable age of ninety-one. Cheerfulness and a gentle temper, which she had shared with him, did not leave her even to the latest hour; but were sustained by the public respect, by the affectionate kindness of her surviving son and two daughters, and by the regard and reverence of all her husband's friends.

I should probably, at some period of my life, have made this sketch of Edward Tilghman, without request, from my admiration of his learning and virtues, and also from the debt I owed him, which has given a zest to every word that I have written of him. He launched me in my profession. I pray to be excused for relating the personal anecdote.

More than fifty years ago, Samuel W. Fisher, the President of the Philadelphia Insurance Company, came one morning into my small office, then having abundant room for all my visitors, and gave me a retainer to argue the case of Gibson against that Company, which I afterwards reported. Mr. Gibson, the plaintiff, who was a member of the Bar, and my master in the law, Mr. Ingersoll, were to argue it against me. The question regarded the proper mode of adjusting a particular average under a clause in a Respondentia Bond; and it was new, and not without difficulty. It came before the Court upon exceptions to a report or award under the Act of 1703, made by Edward Tilghman, with the concurrence of another member of the Bar, against the opinion of the third referee, who was also a member of the Bar; and it turned altogether upon principles of commercial law. I examined the papers, and then said to Mr. Fisher, the President, "You are not going to leave me alone in this cause? You know who is against me?" "I know all that," he said, "but I will not retain anybody else. Go on, and make the best of it." After the award was confirmed, I asked Mr. Fisher why he had been so short in refusing me a colleague. He replied, "that he had done as he was told to do." Mr. Tilghman had told him to retain me, and had said, "Put it on his own shoulders, and make him carry it. It will do him good." The lesson may be good for others. The most cheering effect of it to myself, was its giving me the assurance of the good-will of such a man as Edward Tilghman.

The obituary notice of him which appeared in the newspapers a few days after his death, and which I have said would be allowed to be authoritative when I should name the writer, may very fitly conclude this little memorial. Its author was Chief Justice Tilghman.

"DIED, on Wednesday, 1st November, 1815, in the sixty-fifth year of his age, EDWARD TILGHMAN, Esquire, of this City, counsellor at law.

"Although the usual style of funeral eulogium has almost levelled all distinction of character, yet departed merit has dues which should not be withheld. Mr. Tilghman descended from an old and respectable family in the State of Maryland, and was placed at an early age in the Academy of Philadelphia, where he obtained as good an education as this country could afford. From nature he received a clear and strong understanding, with a disposition for close and laborious study. At school he was distinguished for classical attainments, which he preserved unimpaired amidst the occupations of an active and busy life. The profession of the law was his choice, and his subsequent eminence proved that he had not mistaken his genius. He possessed a deep knowledge of principles, and his sense of duty led him to a thorough investigation of facts, in all his causes. His style of speaking was such as might be expected from his turn of mind—unambitious of ornament, but commanding attention from its intrinsic weight. Regardless of the passions, his arguments aimed at the head, and seldom missed their mark. In stating the evidence, he was remarkably upright; and, on points of law, he gave full weight to the argument of his adversary, and met it without evasion. He never refused a just attention to the opinions of others, however inferior to him; and the unassuming manner in which he delivered his own, gave a character of kindness to his superiority, which conciliated affection, while it commanded respect. To his professional excellence, his brethren of the Bar have recently borne mournful but honorable testimony; and from his example the younger members may derive the useful lesson, that although declamation may glitter, yet success is most surely attained by industry, integrity, and sound legal knowledge. In private life, Mr. Tilghman was no less estimable than in his professional character. His temper was cheerful and benevolent, his friendship warm and steady, and his unshaken integrity has been proved on trying occasions. In the domestic scene his family best know his value. Long will they lament their loss, and never will they repair it."

JARED INGERSOLL.

JARED INGERSOLL.

JARED INGERSOLL, of the Philadelphia Bar, my learned master in the law, was a native of the colony of Connecticut, and was born at New Haven in the year 1750.

His father, of the same name, was a distinguished lawyer in the Colony, and was her agent in England, jointly with Richard Jackson, Lord Grenville's secretary, who was a member of the Parliament which inaugurated Lord Grenville's scheme of taxing the Colonies.

It is to him, the father, that we owe the preservation of Colonel Barré's famous burst of eloquence in reply to Charles Townsend, when he boasted that the Colonies had been planted by England's care, nourished by her indulgence, and protected by her arms, and therefore ought not to grudge a contribution to her treasury. Mr. Ingersoll, who was in the gallery of the House of Commons at the time, immediately wrote out the brilliant reply of Barré, and transmitted it to Connecticut; and from one of her journals it passed into all American hearts, and has become a first lesson in oratory to her sons.

Jackson, and Franklin, and Ingersoll, and all the Colonial agents in England, were opposed to Lord Grenville's scheme of taxation; opposed to it as unconstitutional as well as inexpedient. But none of them thought that the Stamp Act of March, 1765, would be resisted by the Colonies; and Mr. Ingersoll consented even to assist the ministerial plan of distributing the stamps through American agents, to insinuate them the better among the people. He therefore returned to his Colony in August following, with the commission of Stamp-master. But in a very short time he learned something of his people that he had never apprehended before. During his absence, and while the Stamp Act was passing through Parliament, the people from New Hampshire to Georgia had resolved not to pay a stamp tax; and as this was the first assertion of the right by the Parliament of England, had made up their minds to take the Bull by the horns, at all risks.

On Mr. Ingersoll's arrival home, his fellow colonists at first endeavored to persuade him to resign his commission; but he reasoned with them, doubted whether there was anybody he could resign to, doubted if it would be of any avail, and kept them in suspense. He then heard of menaces, extending to property and person, and cast about for protection by the usual means; but, finally, with some astuteness, thought of asking the direction of the Legislature, at Hartford, knowing, that while they liked the Act of Parliament as little as he did, they would as little like to resist it, and therefore might give him their countenance in adhering to his commission.

To attain this end, he left New Haven, as he thought, privately, to put himself and his commission under the direction of the Legislature at Hartford; but his caution was of little avail. That inquisitive and curious people, knew all about his movements. They divined his purpose, and were on the traces of his *incognito;* and, when he arrived on horseback within five miles of Hartford, he found himself riding into a body of five hundred mounted men, who were in something like battle array, though armed with nothing more deadly than staves like broom-handles; and with them he had to ventilate on the broad street of Wethersfield, the definitive question of the commission. This body did not mean that the Legislature should be appealed to on the subject; and, perhaps, the Legislature was very much obliged to them for their intentions. They insisted upon Mr. Ingersoll's resigning his commission on the spot.

The parley was long, but it was vain. It lasted for three hours and more, and neither party convinced the other. Mr. Ingersoll seems to have been as tenacious a reasoner, and as acute, as his son proved to be.

It availed nothing but to show his coolness and skill. At length, when the hours were exhausted, and there were symptoms of impatience, he asked what was to happen if he did not resign; and they told him—"his fate." He might guess what that would be, in the general; but not liking any particular aspect of it, he concluded that it was better to do what he was told to do. He wrote and signed a resignation of his commission as stamp-master. He pulled off his hat, and hurra'd three times for "Liberty and Property," after they had deprived him of both; and then, knowing that he was bound to Hartford, they marched with him to the outside of the Hall of the Legislature, and left him there at liberty to go in, or to go home, as he might think best.

This was the first, and, perhaps, the best conducted case of Lynch law, that our books report. It shed no blood, it broke no bones, and it accommodated the constituted authorities to their hearts' content. The Stamp Act was dead, and the death could not be laid at their door. A striking feature to disprove personal malice on any side was this: that, although affidavits were taken and filed, and some show made of calling out the judicial authorities, Mr. Ingersoll named no names, though he knew the leaders, as well as they knew him.

Such a contest would ordinarily have driven the weaker party into exile, or the extremity of opposition; but in this case it did neither. Mr. Ingersoll, the elder, was loyal to the British Constitution and to the Crown, as were hundreds of thousands of the Colonists in the same day; but he never was a loyalist in the special sense, and his refusal to surrender his commission except by the application of *vis major*, did not alienate the people from him, nor him from them. He remained in his natal homestead; but during the ten years of irritated pride on one side, and of dogged contumacy on the other, which intervened between the repeal of the Stamp Act and the Declaration of Independence, he was more of an observer than an actor; and as, in the later years of that decade, the country waxed more and more warm, and the attention of young men was turning more and more every day to arms rather than to the law, he sent his son, in the year 1774, from the contagious atmosphere of Connecticut, to finish his law education in London.

Mr. Ingersoll, the son, continued in that school until shortly before or after the Declaration of Independence, when he embarked for France, and resided there until the autumn of 1778. From that country to his own, he passed in an American letter of marque, *flagrante bello*, and, as I have heard him say, came pretty much under water, from press of sail, to avoid disagreeable interviews on the way.

His London life, from his own account, as well as from that of Edward Tilghman, his cotemporary for part of the time, must have been pretty equally divided between study and pleasure; though in the allotment for the latter, he included a large portion of exercise on foot. In the summer season he lived in the country, ten miles from his place of study in the City, and not unfrequently footed that interval both morning and afternoon. As a proof of the extent to which females in England use their feet and limbs in the same healthful way, he told me that one of the daughters of his hostess sometimes accompanied him, and, after dropping him in the City in the morning, trotted back with him at the close of the afternoon. The value of that exercise was his frequent theme. He profited by it in his youth, and was able in his old age to dispense with it, by the confirmation it had given to his health. It is as necessary a foundation for a lawyer as his professional studies. Both sexes in our country, and especially in our cities, would take more of it, if our climate, like that of England, and of the Continent generally, would give its more frequent consent; but few of them take as much of it as they might; for to the habitual walker, a cloud is not so often a shower-bath as it is a parasol, nor is the sun so much a scorcher to the quickfooted as to the slow. Next to St. Peter's full ordinance, it deserves universal observance by men of our profession, that " if they will love life and see good days," they must give a fair portion of their practice to their legs. After doing my best, one morning, to overtake Chief-Justice Marshall in his quick march to the Capitol, when he was nearer to eighty than to seventy, I asked him to what cause in particular he attributed that strong and quick step; and he replied that he thought it was most due to his commission in the army of the Revolution, in which he had been a regular foot practitioner for nearly six years.

From relations of friendship between Mr. Ingersoll's father and Joseph Reed, then recently elected a member of the Supreme Executive Council of Pennsylvania, under the Constitution of 1776, and chosen President of that body by the joint ballot of the General Assembly and Council, the son was encouraged by President Reed to remove to Philadelphia for advancement in his profession; and he accordingly removed thither in 1778, was admitted to the Bar in January, 1779, married the eldest daughter of Charles Pettit in 1781, and continued in professional service in that City all the active years of his life, and died there at the age of 72, on the 31st of October, 1822. He had his English education in the law, consequently, some years after he had attained his majority.

Though encouraged to remove to Philadelphia by the President of the Executive Council, and promised his patronage, which no doubt he received as far as it could be afforded, Mr. Ingersoll's success at the Bar, like that of every other lawyer of eminence, was, and must have been, his own work. He received a retainer from the State, during President Reed's administration, as an assistant to the Attorney-General, Mr. Sergeant, in the matter of the Proprietary estates, which were *vested* in the Commonwealth, as the Act of Confiscation calls it, in the year 1779: and the Reports show him to have been associated with the counsel of the State in one or two cases in the year 1780. He was in friendly, and, by his marriage, in family relations, with President Reed, during the three years of his presidency, and until his death in 1785; and was an executor of his will. But President Reed's political ardor during his term of office, and an imbittered opposition to him which had been kindled among men of business and of importance, in Philadelphia, did not make his return to the Bar, in 1781, very easy or agreeable; nor, as I have heard Mr. Ingersoll say, did his mind return willingly to the pursuits of the law. The patron, therefore, must have been more willing than able to assist him; and in a short time Mr. Reed's health gave way, and after visiting England in 1783, he returned toward the close of 1784, and, without attempting to resume his profession, died on the 5th March, 1785. Mr. Ingersoll wanted no other patron than his own talents, learning, integrity, and industry; and if he had wanted any of these, no patron could have raised him to the great elevation which he attained at the Bar.

His professional character, fairly and not partially described, is that of a very sound and well-read lawyer, and a most consummate advocate. Though he was strong as a lawyer in learning, and in the accomplishments which assist the application of it, his great forte was at the Bar, in the face of an intelligent jury, and, indeed, of any jury; and second only to that, was his power with the Court. In his full vigor, which continued for nearly twenty years after the year 1797, I regard him as having been without comparison the most efficient manager of an important jury trial among all the able men who were then at the Bar of Philadelphia.

His priority in this species of service, was, I think, generally acknowledged; and it is my purpose to show, hereafter, with as much brevity as I can, what were the intellectual qualities, and especially the intellectual temperament, which led to this superiority; and how far his falling a little short of this great excellence, in some other exercises of his profession, is traceable to the same characteristics.

He was invited, or encouraged to come to Philadelphia, pretty much under the postulate, that he was to prepare himself for the popular side in politics, which President Reed, in his letter of 3d December, 1778, to Mr. Ingersoll's father, described as not being the side upon which any of the Bar of Philadelphia, who possessed considerable abilities, were to be found. What that side was, in the apprehension of Mr. Reed, it would be useless to investigate in such a sketch as this. The Whig side was, by no means, of one complexion; and among the opponents of President Reed, who was a Whig, were true Whigs whose colors never changed. Some of the features of what he probably regarded as the popular side, were eliminated even in his own time; and if an adhesion to the Constitution of 1776 was the test, it was becoming less and less strong every day, until, with general consent, it was rejected by all, as it was at first rejected by him. A young practitioner of the law, who had gone with ardor into the harness of President Reed during his presidency, might have found himself where the President did at the end of that short career.

Mr. Ingersoll had, at no time of his life, a warm predilection for politics. He had the common aspiration of all patriotic men, after the peace with Great Britain, and the failure of the Confederation, to see the people settled under a Constitution that would build up a Nation, and would promote and secure the public welfare; and, in the general effort to this effect, he took part, by accepting the place of a delegate from Pennsylvania, to the Convention which formed the Constitution of the United States; but, with the exception of this service, from May to September, 1787,

I am not aware that he held or sought a position in any popular or representative body whatever. He was what is called conservative in politics; that is to say, he was not, by constitutional temper, a rebuilder or reconstructor of anything that had been once reasonably well built; nor was his favorite order of political architecture, the democratic. After the great subversion in 1801, he was found as rarely as anybody in Pennsylvania, on the side of the majority. He was known to be inclined to the contrary, so far, that with or without his consent, he was selected in that State, in the year 1812, as the opposition or anti-Madisonian candidate for the office of Vice-President of the United States; but his general course did not manifest a very lively sympathy with extremes in any direction. Mr. Ingersoll's devotion, after I knew him, was to the law, singly and unremittingly, with a decided preference for its investigations and labors; nor did anything, until old age came upon him and impaired his sight, break off or interfere with the great engagement of his life.

He was the first Attorney-General of the State under the Constitution of 1790, and held the office by Governor Mifflin's appointment until Governor McKean's election in 1799, when he retired for, or was superseded by, the son of Governor McKean: and he held the same office by appointment of Governor Snyder, after his election in 1808; and this professional office, and the Presidency of the District Court for the City, for a short time in the last years of his life, were the only offices that at any time drew him away from his extensive private practice. Governor Snyder appointed him without his "application or expectation;" and when in that Governor's last term, the Secretary of State intimated to him that the Governor and others thought that the principal law-officer should reside at Harrisburg, the seat of Government, Mr. Ingersoll replied with great dignity in his letter of resignation in December, 1817, that "the Governor knew the inconveniences of his residence when he appointed him; and that if they had increased, in his own apprehension, he would have saved the Governor the expression of a wish for his resignation; but that, yielding to the Governor's official opinion and authority, he should retire from office, as he entered it, at the Governor's request."

His person, carriage, and manners, and even his dress, had the same aspect in my eyes, and probably in the eyes of all who knew him, from his middle life to the very close of it.

He was of good height, three or four inches short of six feet, spare of flesh, and perfectly well made and erect, expressing much dignity, with the ease and air of good society. His complexion was fair, and his hair light-colored, and his features not large or salient, though sufficiently defined and strong; the lower part of his face, particularly the mouth and chin, being very well developed and expressive. Though to this caste of complexion and features, striking expression does not so commonly belong, as it does to faces in which the features are more irregular, and the shadows deeper, yet nothing could be more manly and clear than the whole tone of his countenance. The perpendicular walls of his head, and the ample roof of the chamber which contained his brain, with the breadth of the lower part of the face, to which I have adverted, gave a very firm and compact appearance to the whole head; and the limner who seized upon these, seized the governing expression of the mass. The best likeness I ever saw of him, was a small and rough pencil-sketch, made by the late Gideon Fairman, while Mr. Ingersoll was addressing one of his most spirited speeches to a jury of which Fairman was a member. He gave it to me, while Mr. Ingersoll's head was yet in the attitude by which the artist was struck. It was produced by a very few strokes of the pencil, which shows, of course, that the head was a speaking one.

His carriage was rather remarkable, and, at this time of day, when familiarity in address and manner is much more common in our courts than it used to be, would be generally remarked. There was a measure, and the observance of breeding in all that he said and did. He was full of attention when you spoke to him, and uniformly regardful of good manners in his reply; but there was little playfulness, no jocularity, nor the slightest attempt at repartee, though he had a keen sense of both wit and humor. When you saw him walk in the street, or pace the floor of the court-room, it was difficult to resist the impression that in early life he had received a military training; and the dress of the pre-democratic age, a full suit of black, or of light brown or drab in the warm season, with knee-breeches and shoes, and long after others had abandoned the usage, hair-powder and a cue, very much assisted the impression. His uniform air of self-possession and purpose, together with the outward attributes I have noticed, gave him decidedly the look of the old officer. But he was entirely free, as the best of that class, of everything like assumption or presumption, or the assertion of command, where it would have been in the least out of place. On the contrary, he gave to every member of the Bar his due in civility and respect, and to those with whom his intercourse was intimate, he was both gracious and cordial.

He passed with some for a rather proud man, perhaps the consequence of this soldierly carriage, and of the forms of life in which he had been bred up, and continued to observe. But the charge in regard to him was even more unjust than it generally is, proceeding as much from that fault in the accuser, as from any serious liability to it in the accused. He had nothing about him, that, in his intercourse with others, whether equals or inferiors, tended to abase anybody. He was not, generally, familiar or communicative. That was the whole. He was not born or brought up in an age in which the worshippers of popularity press hands or lift hats to as many as they can; but he offered and reciprocated civility whereever it was due; and where he professed either respect or regard, he was uniformly sincere. In one sense and respect, he probably was a proud man; and unless we use the word only in the condemnatory sense in which the Scriptures appear to use it, he was none the worse for being so. The purest moralists approve the emotion, though they have not succeeded in giving it a name, by which it may be distinguished from a very different one, of which it bears some of the outward marks. "He had that generous elation of heart, which is the pride of conscious virtue"—virtue in his relations with mankind—virtue that is above the perpetration of a wrong, and spurns a temptation to dishonor. We mean this, when we say that a man's virtue is *lofty*. No man that I ever knew, lived further away from the fault or the toleration of a dishonorable act. His personal virtue was as straight-upward and erect as his person; but he was a religious man also, in open and full communion with the Presbyterian Church, of which he was a member to his death, and made as humble an estimate of his own moral attainments, as if the life he led had been anything but what it was, in close correspondence with his duties.

At one period his domestic relations passed under my own observation, and no one could be more faultless in them. His kindness and even tenderness to his children were striking. Oppressed as he was sometimes with business, and generally obliged to crowd a good deal of it into a small portion of time, I never knew him to be so much absorbed by it, as to make him put aside a request from them, or cut short any of their appeals. I well recollect that on one occasion, when he was instructing me in regard to obtaining some of the means for his preparation in a cause of much importance and urgency, his youngest son, a little fellow of seven or eight years of age, ran into his office with a piece of dough on the back of a fire-shovel, and laying the shovel on the hot ashes, said, "Pa, mind my cake," and ran off to his play. The response was, "*Tsut, tsut*," drawing in his breath with his tongue, "well, I suppose it must be so." This was his usual manner upon such interruptions.

With the world generally, except in matters of business, his intercourse when I knew him first, and I believe afterwards, was not large. His intimate friends were few and select, and, for the most part, such as bore a family relation to him. He was upon a kind footing with all his cotemporaries at the Bar, but not upon an intimate one with more than a very few. He was neither a taciturn nor a reserved man; but was eminently discreet in his language, and said little to no purpose.

After this description, I will state my impression, rather than attempt to give an analysis, of Mr. Ingersoll's mental powers, as applied in both the study and the public management of his causes; though as they exhibit what I think are rather unusual phenomena of the mind, they would probably be worthy of a very full one.

After a long acquaintance with him, and understanding him through his mode of teaching, and by frequently observing him in Court, and in the course of consultations, I came to distinguish between the active and the passive state of his mind, or between its warm and its cold state. The difference may frequently be observed in men; but with him it was so marked, that at times the cold state might have passed for a disruption of continuity between the mind and the faculties. No man was better constituted to show that the mind is a subsisting and organic subject, and neither a mere succession of ideas or impressions, nor a confederacy of independent powers without root in a spiritual body that excites and directs them all. He was a fine practical study for a metaphysician. The intellectual constitution of Mr. Ingersoll, as illustrated in his professional life, proved experimentally to the observer, that although consciousness is the supreme and fundamental faculty of the mind, yet that this, and all the faculties, have their times of somnolency and of sleep, and of waking, renovation, and energetic action; and that they are inherent in a great essence, by which they are stimulated and educated to the work of their several ends, according to their respective nature and use, or to the demands of their work, or of their great motive centre and source.

In what may be called the passive state of Mr. Ingersoll's mind, two or three or more of his faculties would seem to be reposing in it, without giving out any clear evidence of their activity or life. They were, apparently, lying deep in the bosom of their matrix, or like sympathetic ink on the paper, waiting the influence of the requisite heat to make them perceptible; while others would be in a state of gentle action, as if they had not yet gone to sleep, or were just awaking. This was, indeed, the normal condition of his mind in its negative or unexcited state. The law which he had read faithfully, and facts of various kinds which he had collected, would, both of them, be written upon his memory, and would, nevertheless, in that state, seem to have sunk in and disappeared, so as not to be legible, for the time, even to himself. But the moment that the electric flash of excitement passed through his mind, the spiritual body itself would seem to awake; the necessary faculties would wake along with it, and the law and the facts, which had seemed before to have gone from the surface, would stand bright up in the memory, and the influence work from faculty to faculty, with instantaneous quickness and truth. These different conditions of the mind were not made evident by much change of expression in his countenance or person. What it was that specifically put his mind into the positive state, I never ascertained with certainty; but, as I always perceived it, when he was engaged in court, and often perceived the contrary when he was studying or preparing a cause in his office, I inferred that it was emulation or opposition, and, probably, a mixture of both. A particular antagonist might excite him, or the expectation of the Bar in a cause of importance, or the confidence and vivacity of his opponent.

In the negative state of his mind, he did not himself appear to place confidence in the operation of any of his faculties, nor had he his true vigor in either department, whether his memory, his reason, or his imagination; and the latter was as full of activity with him under excitement as either of the other two—not a poetical imagination certainly, which takes its flights into the higher regions of light and æther, but a different form of it, most important for its uses in the Law, where it is an active suggester of relations in life and in the concerns of men, not generally obvious, and is frequently of immense service in the explanation of legal principles, and in the elucidation of facts and evidence. In the proper state of excitement, his mind woke up into immediate energy, and the required faculties sprang to their appropriate work, as if they were new-born, and not merely refreshed by repose. Dr. Reid's remark is no doubt very true, "that the difference of minds is greater than that of any other beings of the same species;" but Mr. Ingersoll exhibited, and illustrated another truth, something akin to that, that the difference of the same man's mind from itself, is, at times, as great as it is from the mind of any other man.

Mr. Ingersoll had a very considerable body of learning in the law, as well as of general information and literature, that was sufficiently at command; and, in ordinary conversation, you did not perceive any deficiency in it; but when he was cold and unexcited, its flow was by no means rapid, and he was not quick to perceive the bearing of what he knew upon the subject presented to him. Very different was the case with Edward Tilghman, who, in several departments of law-learning, not knowing more, and of commercial law knowing perhaps less, brought his knowledge to bear instantly upon the point or points of a case, like a charge of the electric fluid. Mr.

Ingersoll did not open his eyes immediately to the full light that was in him. He would seem to be in that state which the old writers call *darkling*, a diminutive of dark. In this condition of his mind, his faculties would seem not to have light enough to wake them up; and if he then sat down to write an opinion upon a case, he might miss it; and a day afterwards, when something had occurred to put his mind into the proper glow, he would be surprised that he had not before seen, what was then conspicuously clear to him; or if he drew a special plea, or a law-paper which required that he should group all the facts at once, or the principles of law that ruled them, the probability was not small, that, in a different state of mind, he would be the first to find a flaw in it.

In preparing his causes for trial or argument, he seemed to feel this peculiarity, and to provide for it in some degree by the stimulus of motion on the floor, and by suggesting contradictions or opposition on the other side, to work up against them. There was a door of communication between his front and back offices, the upper half of which was glazed like a window, so that what was going on in either room could be seen in the other, though not distinctly heard. No one could have read law with him without perceiving that, in these preparations, he was a complete peripatetic. He would sit for a moment at his table and write, and then would rise and pace the floor, not unfrequently stopping and holding out a hand, or nodding, or shaking his head, and then return to his table, and write again, and so repeat the process for an hour or more, until the work was elaborated; and those who saw his briefs, knew that the labor had not been brief, nor perfunctory. Yet nearly all this preparation seemed to be thrown away, when he got into action at the Bar. He did not resort to his brief with any frequency, and was as clear, and full, and precise, in regard to what had unexpectedly arisen, or been first suggested against him at that time, as he was in regard to what had occupied him in the study. In the vivid state of his mind, he saw and heard everything that concerned his cause, both that which promoted, and that which impaired, his chance of success; and every needful principle of law, with its qualifications, was present to him, all the strength and weakness of his position, all the concessions of his adversaries, however unemphatic or slight, and the minutest facts that were in evidence on either side. But all this time the glow or excitement was in the intellect, and not perceptible in either voice or action.

From these characteristics, it is easy to obtain the reason or cause of his extraordinary excellence as an advocate, and of the shade that sometimes came over its brightness, when he was acting as an adviser or judge. What he did when his mind was cold, was one thing; what he did during the strong action of his mind was another. Though he could not always write off-hand an impregnable plea or opinion, he could criticise it on his legs with the greatest acuteness and strength. His cold opinions had not, by any means, the persuasion or force of his oral arguments. Perhaps he was not so extensively learned in the law of Tenures, and of Remainders, and Executory Estates, as his finished friend and compeer, Mr. Edward Tilghman; yet, even in this line, as Lord Brougham remarks of Erskine, who also was wanting in this and some other kinds of law-learning, "he could conduct a purely legal argument with the most perfect success," by the force of industry previously applied, by the cautious limitation of his positions, which were always taken within the range of his acquired knowledge, and by the bright light of his intellect, which made clear to him the bearing of everything that he said upon the controverted point. But he was most complete and ready, at all times, in commercial law, in which, from his great practice, he was the most frequently called to think and to speak; and which, better than black letter learning, suited the texture of his mind.

When he rose to a Jury, no lawyer could be better prepared with a knowledge of the facts, and of the law that bore upon them; and he chose his point of assault, and his field of defence, with the tact and decision that belong to a first-rate commander. No stratagem of the enemy could seduce him from either. He might be driven from them by force, but not turned by artifice or false attack. His eye was open, and his spirit alert, during the whole contest; and woe betided the adversary that took a false position, or used an illogical argument, or misstated a fact against him. If he felt strong in his case, he might give the error a short correction or rebuke, and pass on to the direct application of his own means; but if he was at all doubtful of his victory, he fastened upon the mistake with the grasp of death, and would repeat and reiterate and multiply his assaults upon it, until there did not remain a shadow of excuse for the blunder. In such a juncture, his having a weak and doubtful cause, it was of no importance to Mr. Ingersoll, whether the blunder was in a material point or not; for he entertained the opinion, and was much governed by it in practice, and was perhaps more than half right in his impression, that if he could satisfy the Jury that his antagonist was decidedly wrong in anything, they would not always distinguish whether it was in the main thing or not. As to catching him in a blunder, material or otherwise, it was out of the question. The thing never happened. He was infallible in every statement he made, whether of principle or of evidence; and the only hope of the opposite side was to show, that what he said might be true, without helping his cause.

He was, moreover, remarkably wary in abstaining from all admissions or concessions that could in any way be turned to his prejudice; so much so, that, before a Jury, I hardly ever knew him to concede or admit anything. This circumstance, undoubtedly, shows the great vigilance that his mind was called to, in the action in which he was engaged. Nothing is more common than for gentlemen of the Bar to endeavor to win upon the Jury by the appearance of candor, in admitting what they think is of no importance at all, to give more color to their sincerity in insisting upon what they deem more important. But Mr. Ingersoll knew its dangers; and without ever being uncandid, he always compelled the adversary to win his cause by his own strength.

He once told me an anecdote that he had heard of Bar practice in one of the States, which, perhaps, had fortified him in his own practice to the contrary. The Bar of that State, as the story ran, were accustomed, when a special verdict, or a case stated, was opened in bank, to relieve one another and the Court, by setting forth, orally, what each admitted in his adversary's favor, and therefore would not be disputed by him. On one occasion, when Judge Chase, of the Supreme Court of the United States, presided, an old lawyer began to state his admissions, and went on with them with some prolixity, Judge Chase taking a note of them for some time, and then stopping. As the old gentleman persevered to make other admissions, the Judge became restive, and at last broke out: "You may sit down, old gentleman; you need not make any more admissions. You have admitted all your case away, half an hour ago." The practice, if it existed, came to an end probably soon after that.

Few lawyers were so facile, plausible, and quick as Mr. Ingersoll was in suggesting distinctions, either in principle, or in testimony, to relieve himself from a difficulty that pressed him; which is also a trait of a quickened mind. And I think we may discover a trace of this talent in the only speech that Mr. Madison records of him, in his Minutes of the Federal Convention; a very short, but, for the occasion, a very fortunate and persuasive one.

There was no question that gravelled the Convention more than the very last they were to decide, namely, in what form or manner the proposed Constitution of the United States was to be attested by the delegates, to give it the best effect with the people.

Almost every delegate of much distinction in the body had objected to some parts of the Constitution; and very few had approved of all its clauses, as well as of its omissions and exclusions.

Those who were most desirous of its success with

Congress and the people, wished an unanimous signature, not for the States only, but by the delegates personally. General Hamilton especially, who, according to Mr. Madison, said that " a few characters of consequence, by opposing, or even refusing to sign the Constitution, might do infinite mischief," expressed " his *anxiety* that every member should sign." " No man's ideas," he said, " were more remote from the plan than his own were known to be; but was it possible to deliberate between anarchy and convulsion on the one side, and the chance of good to be expected from the plan on the other?" I give his language in Mr. Madison's words, without entering into the question of Mr. Madison's accuracy in all respects.

Three prominent members, however, Randolph and Mason, of Virginia, and Gerry, of Massachusetts, had, on the previous day, declared their determination not to sign; and it was apprehended that others reserved themselves for the final action.

Gouverneur Morris had very adroitly put into Dr. Franklin's hands, a form of motion, declaring unanimity in one respect, which it was not easy to gainsay; and, after an excellent speech in his own style, Dr. Franklin moved the Convention, that the Constitution should be signed by the members, and offered, as a convenient form, the words which had been placed in his hands: " Done in Convention by the unanimous consent of the *States* present;" but, in the discussion which followed, Mr. Morris himself, with the view no doubt to gain some of the delegates who might dissent from the form, remarked, that the signing by the members in the form proposed, attested only the *fact* that the *States* present were unanimous.

This very suggestion was the ground of objection by one of the most frank and honorable men in the Convention, Charles Cotesworth Pinckney, of South Carolina; who said that if the meaning of the signers should be left in doubt, his purpose would not be answered. He should sign the Constitution with a view to support it with all his influence, and wished to *pledge* himself accordingly.

This alarmed Dr. Franklin; and though in his written speech he had expressed his desire " that every member should put his name to the instrument," and " that for their own sakes, and for the sake of posterity, they should act heartily and unanimously in recommending this Constitution, if approved by Congress and confirmed by the Conventions," he now said " that it was too soon to *pledge* themselves, before Congress and their constituents should have approved the plan."

Here was a crop of distinctions and difficulties—a pledge to support the Constitution at all events—or a mere attestation of the fact, that the Convention had agreed to it according to parliamentary rule—or a partial signature by the members—or no personal signature at all; and no one could predict the result. Immediately after Dr. Franklin sat down, Mr. Ingersoll rose and said, " that he did not consider the signing either as a mere attestation of the fact, or as pledging the signers to support the Constitution at all events, but as a recommendation of what, all things considered, was the most eligible."

It was at the close of this remark, that the question was taken upon Dr. Franklin's motion; and although the manly aversion of General Pinckney and Pierce Butler to an ambiguous attestation, divided South Carolina, the motion was agreed to by every other State, and every member signed it, Pinckney and Butler included, except the three from Virginia and Massachusetts, whom I have named. And it would have been better if they had accepted Mr. Ingersoll's distinction; for the event has falsified the predictions of the two Virginia delegates; and the Massachusetts delegate, who predicted from the Constitution a crisis in his own State, and spoke of democracy as "the worst of all political evils," afterwards contributed his best to make the Government the thing he had deprecated.

The soundness of Mr. Ingersoll's general positions, with a cautious exclusion of what, though possibly comprehended in them, he did not mean to admit, was one of his forensic characteristics.

His oratory was of a very high order for both

classes of men to whom it was addressed, not varying materially, whether before the Jury Box, or the Bench, except in topics or illustrations. It was clear, earnest, logically connected, rarely or never rising to the highest flights, but always on the wing, not wanting in vehemence on a proper occasion, and always sufficiently animated to keep every one awake. Before the Court his weapons were from the armory of the law and the facts of his case exclusively. Before the Jury he seized with dexterity and effect upon every honest prejudice that could enlist the feelings of the panel. He never stumbled upon an awkward phrase, nor said a bitter thing, nor uttered a pointless expression, nor began a sentence before the thought was ready for it, and the language for the thought. He was not voluble nor rapid. His words did not interfere with each other; nor, in any height of excitement, did his voice bray, nor his arms lash the air, nor his foot explode upon the floor. Neither was he hesitating or slow as if he was inquiring for the next word, nor monotonous as if he was reading from a stereotyped memory. But, with just the proper tone and measure, rising sufficiently above the natural key of conversation to give something like air or rhythm to his language, and speaking as from his brain and not from his brief, he proceeded, with proper pauses and variations of time, from beginning to end, without a single break-down or trip in word or thought.

I have known a distinguished leader in the British House of Commons, utter sentence after sentence with some rapidity, and come bolt up to the last word of his last sentence, without finding it at home. He had to trust, therefore, to a chance selection, and ended in a platitude. This is not, I think, a very common American failing; but the same thing has sometimes happened at our own Bar, and with rather clever men too. But it never happened to Mr. Ingersoll. He was on his feet always, whatever might be the footing of his cause; and his step, whether quick or otherwise, was sustained to the point where he intended to pause. Without affectation of ornament, or the use of coloring words in the place of imagination, he would proceed from hour to hour, if the cause required it, giving out a regular current of pertinent thoughts and manly words to the close. It was impossible for any one to be more clear and intelligible, in the whole design of his speech, and in every phrase of it; and equally impossible, in any part of it, to detect an instance or occasion in which temper, dignity, manliness of carriage, or gentlemanliness of manner, had been either forgotten, or studiously remembered by him, so natural and habitual were these observances with him.

It was not an unfrequent thing with him, to begin his summing up in conclusion to the Jury, with an apothegm, or some historical fact, that was apposite to the main matter, and thus, from the outset, to win the attention of the panel, and assist the impression of his address, by assuming the connection of his claim or defence with an indisputable truth. On one occasion he was counsel for a party who had gone beyond the legal line of retaliation, for sharp words spoken of his mother. "Gentlemen of the Jury," he began, " we are informed by a traveller in Africa, that universally among her savage tribes, they have a saying that is worth our remembering: 'Strike *me*, but do not curse my mother.' The most imbruted negro on the Senegal or Gambia, has this instruction from his wild nature. How much clearer a voice speaks the same language to civilized man, who derives his manhood from the bosom and training of a refined and loving woman! We must take care not to be surpassed in manliness and filial affection by a brutish negro." This is an instance of his manner. It was also, to some extent, the manner of William Lewis. Their practice may recommend it to others; but, unless the speaker has the last word, it is not always difficult to turn an edge of the same kind against him. Mr. Ingersoll, however, was eminently successful at the Jury-bar. I knew him to gain all his causes, and they were many, at a long session held by Judge Washington; and when I reminded him of it, he said: " Yes; I have had good luck." It was the good luck that probably had all the other antecedents to success in a lawsuit, required by Dr. Franklin,—"a good cause, a good lawyer, a good jury, and a good judge." "Good luck" was the Doctor's last requisite.

I have described Mr. Ingersoll's characteristics with the greater confidence and particularity, because I knew him longer and better than any of my seniors at the Bar. I not only read law with him, but, while his powers were still in their vigor, I had attained to practice in that line in which he had held a position of command, and associated him with me as often as I could. I was both happy, and just to my clients, in doing so; for I had great admiration of him, and great confidence in him, and knew both the intellectual and moral foundation on which I reposed. He was a man of the purest honor personally, and of the strictest fidelity in his profession. Both of them, in a general way, were well known to the City; but his honor was more especially known to myself, by circumstances which did not pass to the knowledge of many others. It is rather a singular fact in the history of the Philadelphia Bar, that at least five of its most conspicuous members in his time, came to the close of their business and lives with rather inadequate provision for their families, which, nevertheless, did not proceed from extravagant living, nor from wild and abortive speculation. In three of the instances it might be traced to responsibilities that were assumed for, or cast upon them by, other persons. The carriage of men in the decline of life, under a weight of obligations which must either impair the comfort of their families, or imperil their own integrity, is literally the *experimentum crucis* of their honor; and I do not recollect one of them who did not bear the cross, as their descendants must now rejoice that they bore it.

Our City has one fault in common with all cities, and with mankind in general; and another that is local, and, at this day, rather uncommon. And she has so many good qualities, that she may bear to be told of her defects.

Like all the world, she rushes to the notice of what is new, and puts old merits and services into the wallet, which Shakspeare makes Ulysses say, Time " hath at his back,"

> " Wherein he puts alms for oblivion,
> A great-sized monster of ingratitudes.
> Those scraps are good deeds past, which are devoured
> As fast as they are made, forgot as soon
> As done."

The other is the more uncommon fault. It is not to be regretted that Mr. Ingersoll's day, and that of the really able men who were at his side, was not, in any part of our Country, the day that has since dawned, and it is hoped has got beyond its meridian; a day of puffing and ballooning of everybody and thing, however little above the ordinary stature or quality, sometimes indeed when it is below it. His day was a day of becoming modesty, and of some personal dignity, in all the professions, and nothing will be gained by our day's becoming otherwise. But these qualities furnish no excuse to a great City for indifference to the really great talents that are sometimes found in connection with them. And this is the fault referred to, that she has been hitherto, and perhaps immemorially indifferent or insensible to the abilities of her sons, who have gained their first public consideration elsewhere. She is wanting in civic personality, or what is perhaps a better phrase for the thought, a family unity or identity. She does not take, and she never has taken, satisfaction in habitually honoring her distinguished men as *her* men, as men of her *own* family. It is the City that is referred to, as distinguished, perhaps, from the rest of the State. She has never done it in the face of the world, as Charleston has done it, as Richmond has done it, as Baltimore has done it, as New York has done it, or at least, did it in former times, and as Boston did it, has done it, and will do it forever. She is more indifferent to her sons than she is to strangers; and this perhaps may be the reason why other parts of the State so much more readily advance their own men to public office and distinction.

The fact has been often stated for sixty years past, but is not easy to explain, nor will I attempt to account for it with any confidence. Perhaps it grows out of her Quaker origin. It is certainly in harmony with it, to put nothing more striking than a drab-colored dress upon the men who have done their best for her. It is in the key of Quaker manners of old times—of Quaker moderation and equability. It may, to some extent, be a result of the division of parties in the Proprietary time, the Country against the City, as for the most part adherents of the Proprietary, but with a minority in favor of the Assembly, enough to break their own people into disunion. To this day, the Country of Pennsylvania is against the City in everything, and for no existing cause that can be stated. In recent years, the composition of the City gives the best explanation of the fact; for while there is something like a general temperament in the life and manners of the City, there is no City whose significant population is less homogeneous. We are by no means one, but very many, in origin and education; and not so likely to have a family heart to our distinguished men, as either the South or the East.

But, without explaining it, we may regret it. If it be modesty, it is a virtue that has its inconveniences.

There is no need, certainly, of putting everybody of good figure into scarlet, or flame color, and sending them up by gas, that they may be seen afar; but it is both just to individuals, and profitable to a City, to give to its really able men in every profession or walk, such prominence and decoration, as will bring to both a due share of consideration from the country at large. It helps the community, and it helps the individual. It warms him, and draws him out, or disposes him the more readily to be drawn out. It gives him confidence, and enlarges him both in power and productiveness.

The elder Matthews, an inimitable mimic and droll, at one of his first appearances in the Philadelphia Theatre, when I was present, found his audience rather unresponsive to him. "I tell you what," said he, turning to a group in the orchestra near him, "if you want me to make you laugh, you must laugh at me." This is human nature, and shows that even first-rate talents require the occasional dew of public sympathy and praise.

Full public justice was not done to Tilghman, Lewis, Ingersoll, Rawle, and Dallas, who occupied the front seats at the Bar of Philadelphia, at the close of the last, and the beginning of the present century. It was done at the Bar, and it was done in other States, but it was not done generally in the City. The night is now settling fast upon those memories which go back to their meridian, or even to their declining sun; and this is one motive of my imperfect attempt, in three or four cases, to remove the obscurity that is coming upon names, which at one time, within the halls of the law, were surrounded by as pure a light, and as bright, as is now shining anywhere in any part of our country. One and all of them would have been regarded as able men in Westminster Hall. More than one of them would have stood at the height of that Bar. Their superiors I think have not shown themselves in any part of our land; and among those who have followed on the same spot, the praise of being next after, ought to have satisfied the foremost of them that I have known.

There is another influence that has led to these sketches. Mr. Ingersoll's day at the Bar, was moreover the day of judicial tenure during good behavior. It ought not to be forgotten what sort of men were made at the Bar, by that tenure of judicial office, any more than we should forget who were the Judges that adorned it, and shed their influence upon all around them.

We are now under the direction of a fearful mandate, which compels our Judges to enter the arena of a popular election for their offices, and for a term of years so short, as to keep the source of their elevation to the Bench continually before their eyes. At least once again in the life of every Judge, we may suppose he will be compelled by a necessity, much stronger than at first, to enter the same field; and the greater the necessity, the less will his eyes ever close upon the fact. It is this fact, re-eligibility to office, with the hope of re-election, that puts a cord around the neck of every one of them, during the whole term of his office. It is transcendently worse than the principle of original election at the polls. Doubtless there is more than one of the Judges who had rather be strangled by the cord, than do a thing unworthy of his place; but the personal characteristics of a few, are no grounds of inference as to the many; nor are even the mischiefs already apparent, a rule to measure the mischiefs that are in reserve. We must confess that a system is perilous, which holds out to the best Judge, if he displeases a powerful party, nothing better than the Poorhouse, which a late eminent Chief-Justice saw before him, and committed the great fault of his life, by confessing and avoiding it. The mind of the public, of all parties, is becoming apprehensive upon the subject; and well may it be so, even among party men, for parties change suddenly, and once in every five or ten years, we may be sure that the chalice will come round to the lips of those who have drugged it. No man can be too apprehensive of the evil, who thinks the law worth preserving as a security for what he possesses, and no lawyer who regards it as a security for his honor and reputation. For what can it give of either, if the wheels of the instrument receive a twist or bias through party fear or favor, or are so ignorantly and presumptuously governed, as to let them cut and eat into each other, until they work falsely or uncertainly?

At the formation of the Federal Constitution in 1787, the tenure of the judicial department was thought by our forefathers to be not only the guarantee of that department, but the best guarantee of all the departments of government. What guarantee is there for the Constitution itself, if you emasculate the judicial department, the only one that is a smooth, practical, wakeful, and efficient defence against invasions of the Constitution by the Legislature—the only one that can be efficient in a republican representative government, whose people will not bear a blow, and therefore require a guarantee whose blow is a word? A leasehold elective tenure by the judiciary, is a frightful solecism in such a government. It enfeebles the guarantee of other guarantees—the trial by jury—the writ of habeas corpus—the freedom and purity of elections by the people—and the true liberty and responsibility of the press. It takes strength from the only arm that can do no mischief by its strength, and gives it to those who have no general intelligence to this end, in the use of it, and therefore no ability to use it for their own protection. The certainty and permanence of the law, depend in great degree upon the Judges; and all experience misleads us, and the very demonstrations of reason are fallacies, if the certainty and permanence of the judicial office by the tenure of good behavior, are not inseparably connected with a righteous, as well as with a scientific administration of the law. What can experience or foresight predict for the result of a system, by which a body of men, set apart to enforce the whole law at all times, whatever may be the opposition to it, and whose duty is never so important and essential as when it does so against the passions of a present majority of the polls, is made to depend for office upon the fluctuating temper of a majority, and not upon the virtue of their own conduct?

But an equally inseparable connection or dependency, exists between the Bar and the Bench—between the knowledge and virtue of the respective bodies. A good Bar cannot exist long in connection with a favor-seeking Bench,—a Bench on the lookout for favors from the people or from any one. Such a Bench is not an independent body, whatever some of the Judges may be personally. Nobody thinks it is. The Constitution of 1837, and the people, declare that it is not, by the very principle of the recurring elective tenure. Under a false theory, and for a party end, they meant to make it a dependent body, by abolishing the tenure during good behavior. The Bench therefore as now constituted, is not raised sufficiently above the Bar, to command it by the power of its political constitution. The Bar is constitutionally the higher body of the two, the more permanent, the more independent, and, popularity being the motive power, the more controlling body, though only for its personal and several ends. This is the fatal derangement that the present judicial tenure makes between the two corps. The subordinate becomes the paramount. The private and personal will controls the public; not by reason, not by virtue, not always openly, but by influence.

In our cities and principal towns, the Bar is a large and diversified body. Like the web of our life, it is a mingled yarn, good and ill together; and the ill yarn is not always the weakest, nor the least likely, by its dye, to give hue and color to the whole. Venal politicians—leaders in the popular current—minglers in it for the purpose of leading it, or at least of turning the force of its waters to their own wheels—adepts in polishing up, or in blowing upon or dulling the names of candidates for judicial office—students in the art of ferreting out the infirmities of Judges, and tracking the path of their fears—such men are always to be found in such a body, and to be found in most abundance at the Bar of a Court that has a weak constitution. It is there that thrift waits upon them. There is no need that the pregnant hinges of their knees should be crooked to the Judges, if they only be to those who make them. Where is the independent Bench, that can habitually exercise the restraining or the detersive power, to prevent such "faults" of the Bar from "whipping the virtues" out of Court, or breaking down their influence upon the mass? And if the Bench—not individual Judges—if the Bench, as the Constitution makes it, cannot steadily and uniformly, without special virtue or particular effort, repress the professional misconduct of every member of the Bar, whatever be his popular influence and connections, what honor or esteem will professional distinction obtain from the world, and what sanction will professional integrity have at the Bar?

It is no comfort to think, that the people, or at least a large number of them, must be present sufferers from such a state of things, and that, finally, all of them must take their turn; for the whole people must suffer from a disordered Bar. But the more cutting evil must fall on the honorable members of the Bar, who regard their own distinction in it as an estate in character for those who are to succeed them; and who, if their community be generally vitiated, must see the inheritance of honor which they would lay up for their children, day by day sapped and undermined, while they are toiling against the hour-glass, to find at last in their best acquisitions, nothing better than the sand at the one end, or the emptiness at the other.

The Bar of Philadelphia, I doubt not of all Pennsylvania, but of the former I may speak *scienter*, was, for nearly half a century, under the judicial tenure of good behavior, an honorable Bar, professionally and personally. If there were spots or blemishes, they did not meet the face of the Court, and rarely the face of day. The serene virtue of the Bench was no more disturbed, than its strength was challenged by them. Without any doubt, very many honorable and able lawyers are still extant at it, and so are pure and unterrified Judges. But is there no symptom of change? Perhaps not great. Is the countenance of the public towards the Bench and the Bar the same that it was in times past? Perhaps not exactly. Both the fact and the causes of it are worthy of much observation by the Bar, and by everybody.

Whether the connection between Bench and Bar, however, be such as has been suggested, or the full influence of learned and honorable members of the profession must always be felt, whatever be the tenure of the Bench, in either supposition it must be profitable to lawyers of virtuous aspiration, to recall their predecessors of distinguished name, and to corroborate their own virtue and influence at this day, by examples from the old "good behavior" Bar of Philadelphia.

CPSIA information can be obtained
at www.ICGtesting.com
Printed in the USA
LVHW100826070223
738796LV00006B/940